Rumor Has It

candY APPLe books... just for you.
sweet. Fresh. fun. Take a bite!

The Accidental Cheerleader by Mimi McCoy

The Boy Next Door by Laura Dower

Miss Popularity by Francesco Sedita

How to Be a Girly Girl in Just Ten Days
by Lisa Papademetriou

Drama Queen by Lara Bergen

The Babysitting Wars by Mimi McCoy

Totally Crushed by Eliza Willard

I've Got a Secret by Lara Bergen

Callie for President by Robin Wasserman

Making Waves by Randi Reisfeld and H. B. Gilmour

The Sister Switch
by Jane B. Mason and Sarah Hines Stephens

Accidentally Fabulous by Lisa Papademetriou

Confessions of a Bitter Secret Santa by Lara Bergen

Accidentally Famous by Lisa Papademetriou

Star-Crossed by Mimi McCoy

Accidentally Fooled by Lisa Papademetriou

Miss Popularity Goes Camping by Francesco Sedita

Life, Starring Me! by Robin Wasserman

Juicy Gossip by Erin Downing

Accidentally Friends by Lisa Papademetriou

Snowfall Surprise
by Jane B. Mason and Sarah Hines Stephens

The Sweetheart Deal by Holly Kowit

Rumor Has It

by Jane B. Mason and
Sarah Hines Stephens

CANDY APPLE

SCHOLASTIC INC.

New York   Toronto   London   Auckland
Sydney   Mexico City   New Delhi   Hong Kong

No part of this publication may be reproduced, stored in a retrieval system, or transmitted in any form or by any means, electronic, mechanical, photocopying, recording, or otherwise, without written permission of the publisher. For information regarding permission, write to Scholastic Inc., Attention: Permissions Department, 557 Broadway, New York, NY 10012.

ISBN: 978-0-545-16676-8

12 11 10 9 8 7 6 5 4 3 2 1   10 11 12 13 14 15/0
Printed in the U.S.A.
First printing, January 2010

Rumor Has It

Chapter 1

"Audrey, breakfast!" a voice called up the stairs.

"Coming!" Audrey Jones finished pulling on her jeans and swept her brown hair into a ponytail. A quickly thrown-on pair of socks later, she was skipping down the stairs. She slid into her seat at the table and took a gulp of juice. A stack of pancakes was piled on the plate in front of her, and her mouth was already watering. Her mom's pancakes were the best.

"It's about time, girl," her older sister, Genevieve, said from the seat next to her. "Five more seconds and those pancakes would have been mine."

Audrey knew Genevieve wasn't joking. She

was always first at the table in the mornings and usually had seconds before Audrey had firsts.

"No, mine!" Dorrie, her little sister, countered from the other side. "Mine, mine, mine!"

"I've got some right here for you, sweetie," Audrey's mom said, sliding buttery pieces of cut-up pancake onto Dorrie's plastic plate. "Audrey, could you put the syrup on for her?" Mrs. Jones asked as she went back to the stove.

Audrey reached for the bottle of syrup and obligingly poured a quick stream onto her little sister's plate.

"Can you give me a refill on the juice?" Genevieve asked, lifting her glass in the air and tipping it toward Audrey.

Audrey set the syrup down and, with a small sigh, reached for the carton of juice. She filled the glass halfway and watched her sister take a long sip, then hold out her glass for thirds, which Audrey obligingly poured (while shooting Gen a cold look over the top of the carton).

"Please pass the napkins, Aud," her father said without looking up from his paper.

Audrey closed the juice, passed the napkin holder to her dad, and wished for the hundredth time that her seat was at the *end* of the table. It wasn't, of course. It was in the middle, just like Audrey. No matter how hard she tried, Audrey couldn't escape her middleness.

She was never first, like Genevieve. She was never last, like Dorrie. She was born, and quite apparently destined to remain, squarely in between.

The chicken clock in the kitchen squawked and Audrey's head jerked up. It was almost time to leave for the bus. No time for butter. She quickly poured some syrup onto her pancakes and took a bite. No sooner did the bite pass her lips than she knew it had happened yet again. She'd sat down in front of something warm and delicious, but by the time she actually got to eat, it was cold. Well, not cold, exactly — more like lukewarm. Tepid. Uh, yum.

Audrey told herself to look on the bright side. Her mom was such a good cook that even lukewarm pancakes were better than the breakfasts the majority of her friends ate before school. She knew for a fact that there was a lot of cold cereal and toast going on behind the doors of most middle schoolers' homes — if that.

As if cued from offstage, Audrey's best friend, Carmen Angelo, blew in through the kitchen door with a whoosh of cold air.

"Ooooh, pancakes," Carmen said enviously as she eyed the plates on the table. Her cheeks were rosy from the cold. She was a member of the cold cereal club.

"Here, I've got one hot off the griddle," Mrs. Jones said, slipping the golden brown cake onto a plate and handing it to Carmen. "Audrey, will you get her some syrup?"

"I got it, Mrs. J," Carmen replied, grabbing a chair across from Audrey and reaching for the brown bottle. "Soooo delicious," she said, chewing. "Fluffy, hot, and perfect!" She squinted at her friend's plate through long dark lashes. "Yours are looking a little chilly, Aud." She forked a bite from her own plate and held it out to Audrey.

Audrey leaned across the table and took the offering. It *was* perfect. And hot. She swallowed and beamed across the table at her friend. At least *someone* put her first.

"You girls had better get going," Mrs. Jones said. "The bus will be here any minute."

Audrey shoved the last bites of her cooling pancakes into her mouth. At exactly the same unplanned moment, she and Carmen pushed their chairs back, bused their dishes to the sink, and hurried into the hall.

"Shoes," Audrey said, flinging open the closet

4

door and searching for a pair. The shoe rack was packed with Dorrie's preschool-size Mary Janes and Genevieve's funky flats and chunky boots. Finally, Audrey spotted her own fleecy slip-on boots and tugged them onto her feet. Straightening, she grabbed her jacket off a hanger and pulled it on. A chocolate-brown hat and a pair of fuzzy mittens and she was good to go. "Ready," she announced.

Carmen opened the door, and the unmistakable sound of the bus chugging up the street echoed in their ears. "We're going to have to run for it," Carmen said woefully.

The two friends stepped out into the cold and puffed toward the corner. Their breath turned to clouds of steamy white as they ran, and a thin layer of snow crunched under their feet. But before the chill could slip past their winter coats, they were on the bus and making their way down the aisle.

"You know," Carmen said, gasping for air as she plopped down in their seat, "someday we should actually take advantage of the bus stop . . . you know that place on the corner where we could actually *wait* for the bus to arrive?"

"That would be good," Audrey agreed as she unzipped her jacket. "But at least this way you get some exercise."

"Right," Carmen drawled. "Since only slugs don't go out for volleyball."

Audrey flopped down next to her favorite friend in her favorite seat and grinned. "Exactly!" she said, wishing for the zillionth time that her best friend was also on the volleyball team.

Audrey had been going to school with Carmen since they were six years old, and Carmen suited Audrey to a T. She was not too sweet and not too mean. She was there when Audrey needed her — totally dependable — and never needy or annoying. She had a wicked sense of humor and always knew when, and when not, to crack a joke. Audrey couldn't imagine life without Carmen any more than she could imagine sitting in a different seat on the bus. Which is to say: not at all.

For almost as long as Audrey and Carmen had been friends, they had been sharing the two-rider right smack-dab in the middle on the right-hand side of any bus they rode. Their seat afforded the best views out the windows and down the aisle, and was neither too far forward nor too far back.

Audrey was a middle child, and a middle grader, with a middle seat and a middle-of-the-road philosophy.

Essentially, Audrey was average. Her grades (B's), hair (brown), eyes (blue), and height (five feet), were all in keeping with her above-average averageness. And even though it drove her crazy to be stuck in the middle at mealtime, for the most part being in between was how she liked things. Being average meant she didn't stand out in one way or another. She went with the flow, and things usually worked out all right.

Carmen pushed her shoulder-length black hair back behind one ear and dug through her pack. "Did you get your math homework done?" she asked.

"Of course."

Not standing out also meant not getting in trouble for things like turning in late homework. Audrey slid the assignment out of her folder and handed it to Carmen, who liked to double-check her answers.

Carmen had just located a pencil when the bus brakes squealed and a whoosh of cold air rushed through the open door along with Isabel Collins. Isabel sat down in front of Audrey and Carmen and turned to peer at them over the seat back. "Hi, guys," she chirped, unbuttoning her wool coat.

"Hey, Isabel," Carmen answered through the pencil clenched in her teeth. Then she elbowed Audrey and pointed at number 15 on their homework. She'd found a problem — two answers that didn't match up — and more than likely it was Audrey's mistake. Audrey was digging for her eraser in her pack when the bus lurched to another stop, this one unexpected.

Carmen's papers flew. Audrey grabbed for a loose sheet and missed. When she finally had the escaped paper in her hand, she craned her neck to see what was going on. The bus had never stopped at this corner before, and as far as she could tell there was nothing unusual in the road. She wondered if they had a flat tire. Would the bus driver get off? Would she radio for help? Would they be late for school?

The answer to all three questions was no. Ms. Lester simply reached for the giant lever next to the driver's seat and pulled.

The bus doors swung open. Ms. Lester smiled and a girl Audrey had never seen before climbed up the stairs and paused at the front of the aisle.

"New kid," Isabel hissed.

"Yeah, duh," Carmen whispered back, trying to wipe Isabel's boot print off of her math paper.

Audrey didn't say anything — she just watched as the new girl made her way down the aisle. Every single person on the bus was staring at her, but she didn't flinch. She moved toward them confidently, on long legs. She was tall, probably a sixth grader, and wore a cute polka-dot peacoat and fuzzy knit hat. She met the gaze of each staring student, and when she looked at Audrey, Audrey found herself smiling.

The girl smiled back. Her blue eyes squinched up and she looked genuinely happy — like Audrey had just paid her a compliment. She didn't look at all like somebody facing her first day at a new school . . . midyear.

"Who is that?" Audrey whispered to Carmen, who was still shuffling her mess of papers.

"Dunno," Carmen muttered. "I'm missing a page. Is it under you?" Audrey shifted so Carmen could look, but never took her eyes off the polka-dot girl.

The new girl slid into an empty seat one row back from Audrey and Carmen and across the aisle. If she hadn't been sitting by the window Audrey might have leaned across the aisle to introduce herself. For a second she thought about asking Carmen to trade spots, but a second was all it took for a whole swarm of popular girls from the back to move in.

In an instant the polka-dot-coat girl was surrounded, and the bus was back on the road to school.

Chapter 2

Audrey let her backpack slide off her shoulder and took her seat in homeroom. Mr. Moore liked to keep the desks in a circle, so there was no middle seat in Room 3A. Or maybe every seat was a middle seat, since they all faced the center and nobody was up front or in back.

Carmen plunked her stuff down on the desk to Audrey's right. To her left, Toby Mackenzie was intently erasing a pattern into his dirty desktop. Audrey scanned the room for polka dots and came up empty. Mailee was not there.

Though they had only been off the bus for about ten minutes and still hadn't been introduced, Audrey already knew the new girl's name: Mailee J. Tassle (the *J* was for June), where she lived: Willow Glen Apartments (temporarily while her family looked for a house), and where she had moved from: California (but not LA). Mailee was in sixth grade, just as Audrey had thought. And this just in: She wasn't in Mr. Moore's homeroom.

It was amazing how quickly the kids at Hubert Humphrey Middle School could gather information when it wasn't for a report.

"She's probably in Slatt's class," Audrey said. She didn't realize she'd said it out loud until Carmen shot her a funny look.

"You, too? Jeez, I can't believe how nutso everyone gets when somebody new arrives. I mean, she's just new. She's not, like, an alien or an FBI agent or a rock star or anything."

"I know," Audrey said. As a rule, she completely agreed. It was crazy how new kids became celebrities for their first few weeks at school *just* because they were new.

And yet, for some reason, Audrey was incredibly curious about *this* new girl. If she had been on the cover of *People*, Audrey would buy it, or at the very least read the photo captions while she waited in line at the grocery store. Like everyone else at Humphrey, Audrey wanted the 411.

Luckily, the grapevine at school was better than a gossip magazine and faster than the

Internet. By lunch, Audrey'd gotten a full feed of the latest information. Added to her name, age, and origin, Audrey knew Mailee had tested into advanced math and English and spoke Spanish practically fluently. Her family had vacationed in Mexico over winter break, she played the cello, and her blondish hair was naturally curly.

"So she's good at some stuff," Carmen said when Audrey gave her the report at lunch. She shrugged one shoulder and pulled the plastic wrapping off her straw. "In a week she'll be just like us. Normal." Carmen spoke loudly enough to be heard over the cafeteria chaos. "Just wait and see." She stabbed her milk carton and took a drink.

"I think she sounds stuck-up," Elena Newbold offered. She plopped her tray down beside Audrey and Carmen, who were sitting near the stage in the center of the cafeteria. It was their usual spot and Elena was part of the usual crew.

Applesauce splattered from Elena's tray onto Audrey's hand. She looked around for a napkin to wipe it off and realized hers had fallen on the floor. When she sat back up Mailee was standing at the edge of her table. Audrey felt her cheeks get hot.

"Hi. I'm Mailee. Can I sit with you guys?" she asked.

13

Apparently, she hadn't heard Elena's snotty comment. She smiled just a little and stood holding her tray while she waited for an answer. Elena was silent. Carmen was chewing. Audrey was having trouble talking, but she moved over to make room.

"Sure," she finally squeaked. In her head she was doing a little victory dance — thrilled by this unexpected chance to sit next to the new girl.

Actually, she was completely surprised Mailee would *want* to sit at their table. It was noisy and crowded and none of the popular kids ever sat there — they had their own table by the window. Speaking of which . . .

Out of the corner of her eye, Audrey saw the school-spirit leader, Ginger Stroud, waving from the illustrious window table, obviously trying to get Mailee to come sit with her and the other populars. Audrey considered pointing out the invitation. Ginger was nice enough — she was one of the volleyball cocaptains — but, instead, Audrey pretended not to notice and stared down at her hot lunch.

When she was settled on the bench, Mailee exhaled like she had crossed some sort of finish line. "Thanks," she breathed. "I'll sure be glad when I'm not the new kid anymore."

Audrey was surprised to hear that. From the outside, Mailee seemed to be taking all the attention in stride. But apparently, on the inside, she wasn't loving it. Somehow, knowing that made Audrey like her just a little bit more.

"Heck, I'll be glad when I can find all of my classes. Your school is *way* bigger than my old school in San Francisco." Mailee smiled, and Audrey smiled back. It was cool the way Mailee could make a complaint sound like a compliment.

Isabel leaned in from Carmen's other side. "You're from California?" she asked as if she didn't already know.

Mailee nodded like it was no big deal. "Yeah. My dad got transferred," she explained. "And my mom works from home. So she can go anywhere, and so, well, here we are."

"What's it like?" Elena asked. Audrey gave her a look. She obviously didn't think Mailee was so stuck-up now. "San Francisco, I mean."

"Kinda foggy," Mailee said with a shrug. Audrey thought she was just downplaying. "And I can tell you one thing, winter is a lot colder here," Mailee said with a shiver. She had not taken off her coat or her hat even though the hot dog–scented air in the cafeteria had to be over eighty degrees. "We get some cold weather, but nothing like this. It never snows in San Francisco."

"At least you're prepared." Carmen lifted her chin, indicating Mailee's cute fuzzy hat.

"Yeah, that hat is supercute," Isabel added.

Mailee's whole face lit up. "Thanks! I made it on the drive out. I just taught myself how to knit." She beamed and reached up to touch the downy, multicolored yarn. "I'd take it off to show you, but, you know . . . hat hair."

All the girls nodded and Audrey returned Mailee's smile. She felt oddly tongue-tied and didn't understand why. Thankfully, it didn't seem to matter. She and Mailee grinned at each other for a second until Audrey looked down at her tray. *Definitely not stuck-up*, Audrey thought. In fact, Mailee seemed really nice, like somebody Audrey could be friends with.

"So, is lunch always this good?" Mailee lifted the edge of her bun and peered inside, leaning back a little as if whatever was hiding in the mustard might bite.

"Oh, yes. Just wait for Taco Tuesday," Carmen deadpanned.

"Muy delicioso?" Mailee raised an eyebrow skeptically.

16

"Sí!" Carmen said, giving a wide fake grin while shaking her head no. Everyone cracked up.

"Well then, not everything is different here," Mailee said, still laughing.

Slurping the last of her milk from the carton, Audrey watched Mailee joke easily with the girls around her. She had everything going for her — she was friendly, smart, bilingual, made her own hats . . .

. . . and, Audrey realized, a girl she really, really wanted to call a friend.

chapter 3

The sound of 350 middle schoolers filled the halls of Hubert Humphrey, completely drowning out whatever announcement Principal Sharpe was trying to make over the PA system. Audrey wasn't paying attention to either sound — she was too busy fighting her way up the stream of students to her locker. She had to pick up her gym bag and was annoyed with herself for not taking it with her to science, her last class.

If she had just brought the bag along she would have been halfway dressed for volleyball by now. Instead, she was panicking about being late for check-in. It wasn't the punishment of running extra laps that bothered her either. It was the way the coach said her name when he was irritated.

18

"Audrey! Audrey Jones!" She could practically hear it. Wait. She *could* hear it. Only the voice repeating her name wasn't Coach Markham's. It was Carmen's.

"Here. I grabbed this for you. You don't want to be late." Carmen shoved Audrey's gym bag into her hands. "Thank me later," she said, spinning Audrey around and giving her a shove in the right direction.

"Thanks!" Audrey called over her shoulder into the throng.

At the start of the season, Audrey hadn't really wanted to play volleyball. But her parents had told her she had to sign up for *something* extracurricular. Audrey blamed this on her older sister, Genevieve, who signed up for everything (and was good at everything, too). Audrey's attitude toward extracurriculars — that they really were "extra" — seemed completely abnormal to her mom and dad. They insisted she pick something and stick with it.

So, after a little consideration, Audrey chose volleyball. And the big surprise to everyone was how much she liked it. Just three weeks into the season, Audrey was having fun. Being part of a team felt great, and she got a little bit better with each practice. There was no denying that she was not the best player on the team, but she wasn't the worst, either. Surprise! She was in the middle.

The only bad thing about volleyball was that she missed Carmen. Practice cut into their hang time, and no matter how hard she tried she could not talk Carmen into joining.

"I bruise easily," Carmen said. "I have bad depth perception. I'll break my nose."

Fortunately, Carmen was not opposed to watching the game, just playing it. Audrey could count on her friend to come to games, cheer her on from the sidelines, and — like today's emergency gym bag delivery — help her get to practice on time.

Audrey tossed her backpack full of books into the gym locker, kicked her boots off into the metal closet, and pulled out her practice clothes. She was taking off her jeans when she spotted Mailee out of the corner of her eye, looking chilly in gym shorts and a tank top.

Audrey stopped herself from doing a double take. She felt a nervous surge of excitement like a tiny electric shock. It looked like Mailee was going out for volleyball!

Pretending to focus on her gym clothes, Audrey played with the possibilities in her head. Volleyball would be the perfect way for her to get to know

Mailee outside the cafeteria chaos. There were only eleven other girls on the team, as opposed to 117 girls in sixth grade. Odds were pretty good that they might actually get to talk.

"Hey," Audrey said, trying not to sound as nervous and excited as she felt. "Are you —"

Bang! The door that connected the locker room to the gym slammed open. The two cocaptains, Ginger and Sandy, swooped in dressed in matching maroon-and-goldenrod sweats — Badger colors.

"It's so cool you're going out for volleyball!" Sandy squealed.

"I bet you're used to playing in sand," Ginger added admiringly. Not waiting for an answer, she grabbed Mailee's bare arm and pulled her toward the door. "Come on. We'll introduce you to the team." The three girls walked right past Audrey, who was still shivering in her shirt. Her question was answered — Mailee was going out for the team. But with Ginger and Sandy in the mix, Audrey's chances of getting to know the new girl would be pretty slim. The two cocaptains really knew how to dominate a conversation.

Ginger's loud voice echoed in the locker room even after she was gone. "What's your favorite position? I bet you'll be our new star player. I mean, you're so good at everything."

Cramming her regular clothes into the tiny locker, Audrey slammed it closed and gave it an extra shove to latch it. She felt like she was being squashed into a too-small space herself. Why was she so desperate to talk to Mailee, anyway? Maybe Carmen was right — she'd gone nutso over Mailee's newness. She needed to get a grip.

Wrapped up in her own thoughts, Audrey slouched into the gym. The squeak of gym shoes on polished wood and the echo of Coach Markham's voice snapped her to attention. The team was already doing laps, but her coach hadn't noticed that she was late.

As the girls passed by, Audrey started to run, matching pace with the pack circling the basketball court. The pounding feet provided a distracting rhythm as she slipped easily into a cluster of her teammates. Audrey looked past shoulders and bouncing ponytails to the chatty cocaptains flanking Mailee. The trio was leading the way for the rest of them. As her feet pounded on the shiny wood floor, Audrey wondered what it would be like to be up in front — to be first. You'd certainly be able to see more. But would everyone be waiting for you to set the pace, or challenging your lead and making you go faster than you wanted?

At home, Audrey left it to Gen to be first. Gen was born first, so it sort of made sense that she would do everything else first, too. Of course, being Gen, she took it a little further than just learning to walk and talk and ride a bike before her sisters. She was also the first one picked for any team, the first to cross every finish line, the first to dare do a flip off the diving board, and the first to be cast in the school play (in a leading role, of course). Watching Gen from the bench or the auditorium seat or the edge of the pool, Audrey usually felt grateful that someone else was in the lead. It took the pressure off. But every once in a while she wondered: Was the view better from up there? Was it warmer in the spotlight?

Three laps later, the girls spread out around two nets to do volleys. It was Audrey's favorite warm-up because there were no rules, they just worked together to keep the ball in the air and inbounds.

The white leather balls bounced from girl to girl, never leaving Audrey's sight. They popped over the net and were bumped back. Audrey stepped toward a ball headed her way and let it bounce off of her leveled wrists — only they weren't level. The ball pitched left. So did someone else. Mailee had to knee slide to get low

23

enough to dig Audrey's bad set, but she got under it just before the ball hit the floor.

Audrey stepped back. She was so lost in her own thoughts she hadn't realized that Mailee was playing right beside her — until the new girl kept her bad ball in play.

"Nice!" Sandy yelled from the baseline. Audrey wasn't sure if she was criticizing her or complimenting Mailee. Mailee gave a tiny nod, though — taking the praise. And when she caught Audrey's eye she smiled, just like she had at lunch and on the bus.

"Audrey, heads up!" Nora Oliver, another teammate, called. The ball was still moving and Audrey looked up just in time to see it sailing toward her. Correcting her wrists, she waited, ready to set Mailee up properly this time. All she needed to do was get a good bump. But instead of waiting the right amount of time for the ball to meet her outstretched arms, she swung and smacked it hard, stinging her forearms and sending the ball flying across the gym.

"Oh," Audrey clamped her mouth shut, disappointed, and watched the ball crash into the far wall. "Great." She cringed in embarrassment, certain that everyone was annoyed with her lack of control.

"Wow, you've got a lot of power," Mailee said. She bent to pull up her socks while Terry Griggs chased the ball down at the other end of the gym. "I don't think I could bump that far if I tried."

Coming from anyone else the comment could have been backhanded, but Mailee's smile was genuine. Audrey felt her heartbeat start to go back to normal. Maybe it wasn't as bad as she feared. And maybe she might get a chance to get to know Mailee after all.

The next time a ball came her way, Audrey was truly ready. She bumped and Mailee jumped to handily tip the ball over the net.

"I bet you have a killer serve," Mailee said when they were setting up for a match.

"Sometimes I have trouble getting my serves over," Audrey confessed. She was first up to serve and already feeling a little nervous.

"With your strength?" Mailee looked surprised. "Maybe you just need a better angle. Show me how you do it."

Nervously, Audrey set her feet and tossed the ball. She took a swing and sent the ball in a high arc that came down just on the other side of the net. It went over, but if the other team had been ready they could have spiked the air ball back hard at Audrey's team. Luckily, they weren't set up and returned the ball gently. After a brief volley the ball came back to Audrey for another serve. This time, before the toss, Mailee tilted Audrey's wrist slightly and patted the area that should connect with the ball.

"Try it now," she said encouragingly.

Audrey swung again and the ball flew in a low arc, right over the net before hurtling at an almost impossible angle toward the floor. She'd scored a second point!

The third point was even easier — and proof that Audrey's improved serve had not been a fluke.

"Great job, Audrey," a girl named Lily called from the other side of the net.

"Thanks for the tip," Audrey told Mailee with a grin. She could feel her blood pumping and her smile stretching from ear to ear. And why not? Not only did she have a new, clearly improved serve, she was on the road to making a fabulous new friend, too!

Chapter 4

"So, all she did was just turn my hand a little, like this." Audrey pushed Carmen's fingers closed and adjusted the angle of her palm. "And it was like magic. I mean, I have never served like that before in my life! It was a hundred percent improved. I did it twice in a row!"

Carmen nodded slowly. She was watching Audrey out of the corner of her eye as she slowly pulled her hand away. "You're talking about volleyball, right?" she asked, keeping her voice calm.

"I know," Audrey said, bouncing a little on the bus seat. "I know. It's a weird thing to get all hopped up about — it's just a game my parents make me play and all that. But being able to actually score points is pretty cool. Just wait till you see my new serve. You'll freak."

"Doubtful," Carmen said, slipping down and propping her knees on the seat back ahead of them. "But you never know. After all, Mailee does seem to have magical powers." She waggled her fingers and gave Audrey a half smile before pulling her brimmed knit cap down over her eyes. "Wake me when we get there," she told her, stifling a yawn.

While Carmen closed her eyes, Audrey looked out the window to see if she could spot Mailee at the new stop. Half a block away she zeroed in on her polka-dot coat. With a wave of disappointment she wished she'd thought to switch places with Carmen so she could tell Mailee how excited she was about her new serve — and thank her again for the tip.

Since the end of practice yesterday, Mailee had been on Audrey's mind. There was something really extraordinary about this girl, and it wasn't just that she was cute and smart and good at lots of stuff. She had this way about her — this way of making you feel special, less middle-of-the-pack, but in a quiet sort of way . . . even when you were messing up your volleyball plays in front of the whole team.

When the bus groaned to a halt and the doors opened, Audrey sat up straight so Mailee could spot her. She raised her purple-mittened hand to wave. She'd dug deep in the glove basket to find the mittens her aunt made her two Christmases ago. They were getting a little small and had green thumbs, so Audrey didn't wear them very often. But she figured Mailee would appreciate them since she was a knitter. Maybe she could even teach Audrey to knit so she could make a pair that was all one color.

Audrey watched Mailee squint down the aisle and stomp her feet to get the snow off her boots. Three rows down, Dawn Bender was waving madly and patting the seat beside her. Audrey was sure she heard Sandy calling Mailee's name from the back, too. Mailee didn't look any farther than Dawn, though. She plopped down with a smile on her face like they'd been friends forever.

Audrey's hand sank back to her lap and she pulled off one of her mittens by a green thumb. She wondered if she was being as goofy as Dawn with her waving and grinning. Dawn didn't have lumpy hand warmers on, and she wasn't on the volleyball team. Still, Mailee had flashed the girl her winning smile and sat down right next to her. Now the two were talking and laughing.

29

Maybe Mailee wasn't singling out Audrey with her volleyball tips and her friendliness. Maybe she didn't think Audrey was exceptional or great friend material. From the looks of things, Mailee was just that nice . . . to everyone.

The weird thing was, the more Audrey thought about how nice Mailee was to everyone, the less nice she felt. The corners of her mouth began to feel heavier and edged down toward her chin. Her feet grew heavy, too, so that it felt like her shoes had been filled with concrete as she dragged through the morning.

Audrey had woken up wishing that volleyball practice happened every day so she could try out her new serve again and again and again. Now she was glad the team had Tuesdays and Thursdays off. She did not want to be near Mailee with her bad attitude and leaden feet.

"You okay?" Carmen asked in the lunch line.

Audrey could only shrug. Technically, she was fine. She felt cruddy, but when she thought about how she might explain her feelings to Carmen it all sounded completely lame. She could say:

You see, I thought I was special — special enough to hang with the new girl. Lame.

I was hoping Mailee would say hi to me on the bus. Lamer.

When Mailee taught me to serve better I thought she actually wanted to be my friend. Lamest.

Mailee had just given her a volleyball pointer — nothing more. But she did not want to feel any stupider than she already did! And having Carmen accuse her of catching new-kid fever when she tried to explain would definitely make her feel worse. So she just followed Carmen back to their table without saying a word and wedged herself in between Carmen and Isabel at the end of the bench.

She stared glumly down at her Tuesday taco. She wasn't very hungry, and the meat looked even weirder than usual.

"Muy delicioso?" came a voice from the end of the table. Mailee stood with her own Tuesday taco, grinning down at the girls. Carmen and Isabel laughed.

"Here, we can make room," Elena said, sliding over.

Audrey turned, stunned, toward the window table to see if Ginger was waving Mailee over. Maybe now would be a good time to point out other seating options. But Ginger was busy eating her yogurt and laughing with her friends, and Audrey didn't feel like speaking up and telling Mailee she was at the wrong table. Instead, she took a big bite of bad taco and hoped the rest of the school day would pass quickly.

Sadly, being at home didn't make Audrey feel any better. She had a lot of homework to do, but her sister Gen had spread out all over the dining room table (where Audrey usually did her homework), working on some posters for the school play. And when Audrey tried to tackle her math problems at the kitchen table instead, her little sister, Dorrie, wanted to "help."

"Mom, she's drawing on my paper," Audrey complained. A bright purple crayon mark snaked its way across her math and onto the wood surface.

"Oh, Dorrie, no crayon on the furniture!" their mom scolded.

Grabbing up the toddler, Audrey's mom let out an exasperated sigh. "Why don't you do your homework in your room? You have a perfectly good desk in there."

Fine. Audrey stomped upstairs to her room, where she sat alone, banished and unable to think. Outside, her dad was scraping the icy walk. She could hear the shovel grate against the frozen snow while her unfinished homework taunted her from her desktop. It didn't seem humanly possible for her to feel any more irritated when her misery was rudely interrupted.

"Hey, do you have any nail polish remover?" Gen asked, waltzing in without knocking.

Even though she didn't want to be alone, Audrey felt her annoyance flare higher than ever. "Hello? My door was *closed*," she snarled.

"Yeah. Sorry." Gen knocked on the wall. "So, you have any nail polish remover?" She was inspecting her newly polished nails on her left hand. "I'm all out and this blue just looks nasty next to this green. I think it should be black next, then green." She turned her hand so Audrey could see.

Each of Gen's fingernails was painted a different color, and in Audrey's opinion they all looked nasty next to each other. But Audrey was not really a nail polish kind of girl, and she was definitely not a multicolored nail polish kind of girl. The farthest she went down the glossy lacquer road was to paint her toenails with Carmen, and that was generally a sleepover thing.

"No. I don't have any," Audrey answered. "Now go."

"You sure?" Gen opened Audrey's top dresser drawer and began to rifle through it with her unpainted fingers.

Audrey gave up with an exasperated sigh. "Fine." She got up to help Gen look. It was, she hoped, the fastest way to get rid of her. "Here." She located a tiny bottle of remover behind a stack of books on her dresser and handed it over.

"You're a doll." Gen beamed, then stopped and looked at Audrey, really seeing her for the first time since she barged in. "What's up with you?" she asked. "You look wrecked."

Normally, Audrey would go to Gen for advice right after she asked her neighbor's shih tzu, Cocobunny. That is to say: never.

The sisters were so different that it simply didn't make sense for Audrey to ask Gen about . . . anything. But for some reason, call it desperation, Audrey let it out.

"What's the best way to determine, you know, secretly, if someone might like you?"

Gen's jaw dropped and her eyes bugged out so far she looked a lot like Cocobunny the shih tzu. She reached up to touch her forehead in shock and almost touched her hair with her wet nails.

Seeing her sister's reaction, Audrey wished she

could pull the words out of the air and stuff them back into her mouth.

"Oh my gosh! Oh my gosh! You're in love!" Gen squealed, flapping her wet fingertips. She sat down on Audrey's bed for a second, then bounced back up. Climbing onto the white cover with her Converse still on, she started jumping like those people on TV when they win the lottery.

"Oh my gosh, this is so great," she burbled. Then, suddenly, she came to a standstill. Her eyes were about to pop out of her head. "Who is he?" she demanded. "You have to tell me."

"It's not what you think," Audrey said firmly. It was obvious she'd made a huge mistake, but there was no turning back now. "I am not in love. I don't even have a crush. I'm talking about a friend."

Gen was sitting down now but still gazing intently at Audrey.

"There's this new girl at school," Audrey explained. "I can't explain it, really . . . I just think she's super nice."

"It's not just a new-kid thing?" Gen asked skeptically.

"No." Audrey shook her head. She could just hear Carmen saying the same thing. But it was more than that, she was sure it was, even if she couldn't really explain why.

"Okay," Gen said, sitting up a little straighter and taking the matter seriously. "Let me think." She unscrewed the top of the nail polish remover, tipped the bottle onto a cotton ball she had stuffed in her jeans, and started removing. "Well, there was this one time when I really wanted to know what Tim Galloway thought of me. . . ."

The sharp smell of acetone filled the room, but Audrey barely noticed. She was all ears.

chapter 5

Audrey couldn't believe that Gen had any interest in helping her with her problems — her big sister usually treated her like cold leftovers. Still, by the time Gen was halfway through her story, Audrey knew her sister's advice didn't apply. There was no way Audrey was sneaking into the school bathrooms and writing on walls. Repeat: no way.

As her sister tossed the polish-stained cotton ball into the wastebasket, Audrey sighed. She should have known that asking Gen wouldn't help — they were too different. And yet, when Gen wrapped an unpainted hand around her shoulder and gave it a squeeze, Audrey felt a tiny bit better.

"You just need a Sharpie and a hall pass," Gen finished.

Audrey was tempted to tell her sister that she was bonkers but didn't. After all, she was only trying to help. "I'll consider it," she fibbed as she put the cap back on the nail polish remover.

During dinner — while she absent-mindedly directed the dish traffic over her fast-cooling food — Audrey found herself thinking about her sister's bold actions. Writing on bathroom walls was not for her, but she had to admit that Gen had gotten the answers she was looking for. In fact, she and Tim Galloway had dated for three months and were still good friends. So, even though the graffiti method wouldn't work in her case, it proved that it was possible to find out what some-one thought about you without letting him or her know you were fishing.

As the idea seeped into her brain, something else began to seep into her sleeve: Dorrie's milk. The toddler was shaking her sippy cup so that it created a small stream that ended in Audrey's cuff.

"Dorrie!" Audrey cried in alarm. She jerked her hand off the table, spraying milk.

Immediately, Dorrie began to wail. Gen cracked up and their mom jumped out of her seat and snatched up Dorrie to comfort her. "It's just a little spill," she crooned, giving Audrey one of her scolding looks.

Before Audrey could explain, her dad had the milk cleaned up, Dorrie's cry had turned to a whimper, and Gen had taken over the conversation — treating them all to a list of reasons why she was going to get the lead in the upcoming production of *Guys and Dolls*. It was over, and somehow it had all been Audrey's fault. Caught in the middle again.

Audrey looked at her green beans, tuning Gen out. And then, as she was swallowing a bite, she got an idea. It was a little reckless and a lot against the rules. But it didn't involve sneaking around the school or making extra work for Mr. Harrison, the janitor. In fact, Audrey could set her plan in motion in the privacy of her own room. . . .

"Can I be excused?" Audrey asked. She gulped down the last of her milk while she waited for an answer.

"Of course, sweetie," her mom said, distractedly cutting up some chicken for Dorrie.

Audrey cleared her plate, loaded the dirty dishes into the dishwasher, and headed up to her room. Pulling a new notebook — the one she'd bought for English class — out of her bedside table drawer, she propped it on her knees and gazed at the cover. Then she grabbed a package of markers and opened the notebook to the first page. Smiling to herself, she wrote two little words: *SLAM BOOK*.

A tingle went up Audrey's spine as she flipped forward a few pages and started adding entries. She began with the basics — a section on "who's got the best _____," which included eyes, hair, smile, clothes, name, vocabulary, ideas, and chance of becoming president.

Next, she created a section on favorites — movie, dessert, jeans, magazine, actor, song, and animal. She made another section for least favorites — vegetable, toothpaste, subject, parental expression, hot lunch item, household chore, celebrity.

The third section was a bunch of "either/ors" — Pepsi or Coke, vanilla or chocolate, summer or winter, sweet or sour.

She peppered in a bunch of short-answer questions and fill-in-the-blanks, skipping pages and flipping back so there would be extra room.

They're innocent enough, she told herself as she spaced out her entries and left pages blank for new additions. Then she turned back to the front of the book and hesitated. She knew she wanted to lay down some ground rules for writing in the book, but what were they?

Audrey tapped the pen against the blank page. Then, after several minutes of brainstorming, she began to write.

When you write in this book you must do it by yourself — no team writing.

1) *Choose a number.*
2) *Write your answer next to your number on each page.*
3) *Put your name beside your number at the end.*
4) *Add a new entry when you have finished filling them all in.*

The more she worked, the more excited she got. She could picture her classmates writing in their answers and giggling over other people's.

And most important, she could see herself actually finding out what Mailee thought of her. . . .

Taking a deep breath, Audrey turned to a random page in the middle of the book and wrote one last entry — a fill-in-the-blank: *Audrey Jones is* _____.

Gazing down at the page, she could feel her face flush. The prospect of finding out what Mailee thought of her, or if she even thought of her at all, was so enticing she could barely contain herself. This was the perfect plan!

But perfect plan or not, Audrey still had homework to do. She stuffed the slam book into her backpack and pulled out her science text. Cell parts swam before her eyes for almost half an hour before she buckled down and really got to work. By the time she started on her last question, it was nine fifteen and the phone was ringing. Audrey dashed into the hall, looked at the caller ID, and grinned. Carmen.

"Hey, girl, how's that math?" Audrey asked, padding back into her room and closing the door. She slid her science book off her desk and slipped it into her pack. She could see the green corner of her slam book sticking out and pulled it onto her lap. Maybe she should tell Carmen about it. . . .

"I just finished," Carmen replied. "But I think Ms. Palmer is trying to kill us. It might be time to notify the police."

"It's definitely a plot. Middle school teachers think it's their job to torture their students," Audrey replied with a laugh. "It's in the teacher code or something. But, I'm sorry to say, I believe it's perfectly legal. In fact, it may be mandatory."

Carmen chuckled. "You're probably right. But I didn't call to complain about math. I've got some exciting news!"

"Tell me," Audrey said, thinking about her good news, too.

"I need you to come shopping with me tomorrow after practice. I just got my allowance and I have enough for those cool jeans we found at Carpo's. My mom even said she'd drive us."

Despite the fact that they had totally different styles — Audrey was a comfy tee-and-basic-jeans girl, and Carmen went for maximum embellishment and color — the two girls made an excellent shopping team. They had found Carmen's dream jeans — a bright over-dyed turquoise pair — on a mission a few weeks before. "Enough money and a ride — that *is* excellent news," Audrey said.

"I know, right? And I want to get there before they run out of my size or something," Carmen said. "So are you in?"

"I'm in," Audrey confirmed. Underneath her desk she ran her hand over the cover of the slam book. She was dying to tell Carmen about it but stopped. The whole plan would have more impact if she waited until the morning so she could show it to her at the same time. "I'll come over as soon

43

as practice is finished," she said. She glanced at her favorite worn sweatshirt with its now milk-crusted cuff. "Maybe that hoodie I wanted will be on sale."

"Fab. And while we're — oh, hey, I've gotta go. I forgot. Mom called a family meeting."

"Is everything okay?" Audrey asked. *Family meeting* was the term parents used for "we have something to discuss that you are not going to like." She could hear Carmen's mom yelling for her in the background.

"As far as I know," Carmen replied. "August is probably forgetting to rinse the dishes before he puts them in the dishwasher or something. You know how my mom is about her new dishwasher. . . ."

"Yes, I do," Audrey admitted with a grimace. There was practically a flow chart for loading that thing. "If you want some of my mom's French toast tomorrow, you should come a little early," she advised. "My sisters can wolf down a whole loaf's worth in record time."

"French toast. Yum." Carmen smacked her lips. "I'll be there."

As she hung up the phone, Audrey promised herself she was going to do two things: 1) get to the table early so she could eat something warm and 2) play it cool with the newly created slam book.

She hoped she could pull off at least one of them.

Chapter 6

"I can't believe you missed French toast day!" Audrey said as she pulled off her jacket and hung it on the center hook in their shared locker. "It was amazing." She had made it to the table a full minute and a half before Gen and had eaten half a slice in relative peace. Also amazing.

Carmen stifled a yawn and lazily peeled off her red winter jacket amidst the mass of middle schoolers arriving for first period. "I know, total bummer," she agreed. "But I couldn't get up this morning —"

"You sound like me!" Audrey interrupted with a laugh. She'd managed to keep one of her promises to herself but was not ready to confess that one of the reasons she hadn't overslept was because she'd barely slept at all. Twice in the night she had turned on the light and stared at the slam book, barely believing she had actually come up with such an out-there plan. She was such a jangle of nervous energy she felt like she might at any moment do one of two things: 1) bolt out the school doors and bury the book in her backyard next to her dearly departed hamster, Frankenstein, or 2) get on the PA system and let everyone know that her brilliant creation had arrived at Humphrey. She did neither, of course.

What she did do was pull her secret notebook out of her backpack and tuck it under her arm while she swung the half-empty bag into the bottom of her shared locker.

"Tomorrow is oatmeal," Audrey said, stepping back to let Carmen unload her homework. "Not that exciting." She yawned in spite of the adrenaline coursing through her veins. Just bringing the slam book into the light of day made her heart race.

"Right," Carmen agreed. "But it beats Kix on a winter morning for sure." She gave a sleepy half smile and pulled a couple of books from her bag. Carmen was more tired than usual today, too. And grumpy. She had spent the entire bus ride doing homework so they barely had a chance to talk.

Audrey figured the Angelo family meeting must have gone late but knew better than to grill Carmen about it. Her best friend liked to get to things in her own time. She claimed she needed to process before she could download. Sometimes she could get in a quiet mood for hours — or even days — and Audrey was okay with riding it out.

Only today she didn't have a lot of time.

Audrey glanced at the book in her arms. It was now or never. She hoped her best friend would be as excited as she was, that she would really like it and think it was fun. But she also worried that Carmen, who knew her better than anybody, would know immediately why she made it and think it was dumb. She could already hear her saying, *I can't believe* you *of all people are falling for this whole new-kid mystique!* And she knew she wouldn't be able to explain why becoming friends with Mailee was so important. . . . It just was.

Steeling her nerves, Audrey closed the door of their locker around them a little and leaned in closer to her friend. *Grumpy or not, here I come. . . .*

"Hey, can I have a little space? I'm trying to get organized here," Carmen griped, opening the locker door wider.

48

"Okay, cranky, I just wanted to show you something," Audrey whispered, leaning in again.

Carmen glanced over at the book in Audrey's hands and looked at her as if to say, *Yeah? And?* When Audrey opened the book and showed her the title her friend's expression changed completely. Carmen's eyes went all buggy and she dropped her pack into the locker with a thunk.

"Is that what I think it is?" she whispered, staring at the eight block letters on the page in front of her. "Holy baloney. Did you make this?"

Audrey nodded.

"Audrey, are you crazy? Slam books are against the rules. *Seriously* against the rules. The last person who got caught making one of these things got suspended for a week and had to write a letter of apology. It was printed in the school paper! How could you, of all people, forget that?"

A wave of disappointment practically knocked Audrey over. On a good day, Carmen was the spunky one of the pair, the one who liked to mix things up. Where was her sense of adventure?

"I didn't forget," Audrey said defensively. "I'm just planning on not getting caught."

Carmen was still looking skeptical. Very skeptical. "You hate getting in trouble," she whispered.

"It's your worst nightmare. I mean, you? In the principal's office? I don't think so."

"Stop being such a worrywart. It's just for fun. Nobody will ever know who started it. And besides, my entries are totally harmless." Audrey pulled the door in closer and flipped through a couple of pages to show her friend.

Carmen took the book out of Audrey's hands and skimmed a few "least favorite" pages, muttering something about having had enough shocks to her system lately. Then Audrey watched her crabby face change as she got sucked in. "Oooh, I hate eggplant," she announced. "Can I be lucky number eleven? Where's my pen?"

Carmen knocked the locker door open wide and crouched down to search for something to write with. She felt around with one hand while the slam book flailed in the other.

Audrey pulled the door back around and scanned the hall to see if anyone was paying attention. Luckily, nobody was at the lockers on either side of theirs, and the hall was starting to clear out as kids headed to homeroom.

"This is actually really cool," Carmen said approvingly, still reading and hunting for something to write with at the same time. "Kind of like a memory book. Oh! And there is nothing more disgusting than bubble gum–flavored toothpaste. I mean, it doesn't even taste like bubble gum, and after you brush it's just . . . blech. I swear I put my pen in here. . . ."

Panic started to rise in the back of Audrey's throat and she held her own pen behind her back so Carmen wouldn't see it. "Carm, I really need to keep this on the QT!" she whispered loudly.

A group of girls was rounding the end of the row of lockers and coming their way. Maybe it was Carmen's reaction — telling Audrey that making a slam book was totally out of character — but Audrey was suddenly terrified of getting caught.

"You can add your entries later," Audrey told Carmen, gently extracting the book from her friend's hands just before the other girls passed by. "If you go first everyone will know I started it," she explained. Carmen looked disgruntled.

I'll tell her later, Audrey promised herself, trying not to feel too guilty about not spilling the rest of the story. *Right after I find out what Mailee thinks of me.*

"So, *now* all of a sudden you're worried about getting in trouble?" Carmen asked.

The bell rang, echoing off the walls. "Uh-oh. We're going to be late if we don't move it," Audrey pointed out. She pulled Carmen to her feet and Carmen closed the locker door with an annoyed bang.

Carmen's excitement about the slam book disappeared as quickly as it had appeared. Her grouchiness was back, but so was her sense of humor. She pulled the hood of her sweater up so it shaded her eyes, held out her arms zombie fashion, and let Audrey lead her down the hall like she was Audrey's very own mad creation. "Yes, Master," she droned.

"This is our secret, okay?" Audrey said, tugging Carmen toward homeroom class.

Carmen nodded from the dark of her sweater. "Yes, Master," she said again. Then, dropping the monster act she added, "Just promise me you'll save line number eleven for me. I could use some luck."

The two girls walked faster and faster, dodging seventh graders. Audrey scanned the crowd.

"Oh, and speaking of secrets," Carmen leaned closer, "I almost called you back last night —"

"Hold that thought," Audrey interrupted. She'd spotted what she was looking for. Melissa Valoria was wandering up ahead. Totally scattered, Melissa usually daydreamed her way down the hall with her bag wide open. This morning was no exception. Her monkey-print duffel yawned wide, one strap flapping by her knee. It would be easy to grab a notebook from the mess inside or drop one off. . . .

"I want to get this started before homeroom," Audrey whispered. "This little book is in for one serious adventure!"

Chapter 7

Audrey tapped her pencil on her desk and grinned as she watched a folded piece of paper move stealthily from one student to the next. It was the third note she'd seen this period. Luckily, Ms. Mulroy had spent most of English class busily writing her own notes — the ones her students were *supposed* to be paying attention to — on the board. She had no idea that additional information was circulating behind her back.

Someone passed Audrey a note and she quickly unfolded the paper before passing it on. *Slam update: Jed Brockett likes brunettes better than blonds, and Julianne Hastings hates ice cream —* all *flavors!*

Audrey tried to act casual as she read the paper, folded it back up, and passed it to Alice Austin. Who knew that creating a buzz would be so easy? The only thing she'd done (besides making the book, of course) was to slip it into Melissa's bag before homeroom. Sure, she'd had to do it without getting caught, but that had taken about a second and a half. And now the whole sixth grade was talking about *her* slam book!

It was a little surprising to Audrey how much she wanted to tell everyone that the book was her brainchild. Since when did she like to be the center of attention?

Did it start with those improved volleyball serves? Mailee's encouraging smile? Meeting someone who was nice and just a little bit quirky? Audrey wasn't sure. She just knew that this was one secret that was seriously hard to keep.

Still, she was determined to keep her hand in it on the down low, at least for now. Her creation wasn't making the rounds just for fun. It was the essential tool of an urgent mission — a mission to find out if she had a new friend (or the potential to make one) . . . or not.

It'll only be a little while before the book lands in Mailee's backpack and I'll have all the answers I need, she told herself. After that, everyone in Hubert Humphrey Middle School would be free to find out how brilliant Audrey was.

The final bell rang and, armed with her practice gear, Audrey headed to the gym to change. She kept her ears open for any new gossip and an eye out for Mailee as she hurried along. She wondered how many people had filled out the book so far. Five? Twenty? It was clear that more people knew about it than had actually written in it. Everyone, it seemed, liked to take his or her time, reading it through and making his or her answers as funny as possible. And the longer it circulated, the longer it got and the more time it took to read. Filling it all in was starting to take more than a morning break or fifteen-minute in-class, home-work-time commitment.

Audrey was so lost in her thoughts about the book she didn't realize she was the last one in the locker room until she heard someone call her name.

"Audrey, hurry up!" It was Sandy, one of the cocaptains. "Everyone else has started laps."

Audrey heaved a huge sigh, slammed her locker shut, and hurried into the gym. Sure enough, the girls were already halfway around the court, ponytails bouncing.

Audrey sprinted up to the pack, settled in just behind Mailee, and circled the gym with the rest of the team. Coach Markham was staring hard at his clipboard, and she hoped her tardiness would go unnoticed for the second day in a row.

No such luck.

"Jones and Whitney, take two extras," Coach called out.

While the other girls settled in for volleys, Audrey and Lily Whitney circled the track.

Audrey could hear Lily panting beside her and knew this was her chance. "Did you hear about the —"

"No talking!" Coach called. He was all business, Audrey realized. There'd be no gossip today and no finding out if Lily knew which girls on the team had gotten a turn with the slam book.

During volleys, Audrey tried to concentrate on her wrist position. She got in a couple good bumps, but mostly it was luck. She was too busy wondering if Mailee had seen — or even heard — about the slam book yet to keep her focus.

"Keep those balls in the air," Coach Markham bellowed from the sidelines. "I don't want anything touching the ground except your feet . . . or your knees if you go for a slide."

"Nice one," Ginger told Mailee as she spiked a ball over the net.

"Thanks!" Mailee grinned at the compliment and kept on playing, gracefully diving for another ball. She nailed it, and Audrey watched as it arced back up and over the net, landing in a dead spot. The girl was phenomenal.

Audrey tried to show Mailee how her tips had improved her game by acing her serves. During the matches, she managed to score a few points in spite of her half-absent brain and even dove a couple of times to successfully keep the ball in play.

"Nice job, Audrey," Sandy said approvingly. "You're really getting the hang of this."

Audrey beamed. For the first time all season, one of the cocaptains had complimented her play. She was improving! And it was all because of Mailee. . . . Audrey thought some of her quiet magic must be rubbing off.

The whistle blew. "Quick cocaptains' meeting," Coach Markham called out. "Everyone else, you're done for the day."

The girls headed into the locker room to slip

back into their school clothes and gather their things.

Audrey wanted to thank Mailee, but out of Coach's earshot, the team started chatting up a storm. Audrey could barely get a word in.

"I've heard the diner on the corner serves a mean hot chocolate," Mailee said. "Does anyone want to get one?"

A chorus of yeses echoed in the metal-furnished room, and Audrey felt a little chill of excitement. Terry had to go to the orthodontist and Anna's mom was picking her up, but six of the girls were going. In the group (and away from the coach), Audrey thought she might be able to find her voice and a discreet way to ask Mailee if she'd seen the book yet. And even if she didn't, a cup of whipped, creamy hot chocolate sounded great! With Mailee leading the way, she and the other girls made their way out the door.

Fifteen minutes later, the six girls were squished into a booth by the windows at the Easy Street Diner. The glass to one side of the table was quickly steaming up, thanks to the giant mugs of hot liquid sitting in front of them. Audrey was squeezed in beside Mailee and feeling fabulous.

"Whipped cream, anyone?" the waitress asked with a grin. She tipped the big silver spray can over each mug and added a little white mountain to the top of each one.

Make that extra fabulous.

Audrey spooned up a bite of fluff and swung her feet a little under the padded bench. Across the table, Elena's face was covered by her un-ponytailed hair as she rummaged around in her striped messenger bag. Two seconds later, she pulled out a green notebook — the slam book.

"You guys. Check this out." She put the book on the table. "Have you seen this?" she asked, her eyes bright with mischief.

Audrey stopped breathing.

Nora leaned in for a better look. "Is that *it*?" she asked, her eyebrows practically touching her hairline.

"The one and only," Elena replied with a little intake of breath.

"What? What is it?" Mailee asked. She was wearing a striped scarf, and as she talked, she unwound it from her neck and reached across Audrey to hang it on the hook at the end of the bench seat.

Audrey forced herself to begin breathing again before anyone noticed. Her feet were frozen mid-swing and she hoped she did not look as star-tled as she felt. *Act normal*, she coached herself. *Don't give it away!*

Yes, she wanted Mailee to find out about the slam book. But not like this! Audrey wasn't sup-posed to be anywhere nearby when the book came around to Mailee. What if everyone started paging through it and found her name and her entry right smack in the middle?

Stay calm, she told herself firmly. *They have no idea that you started this, or why.* Still, she could feel her face getting warm.

"It's a slam book!" Nora blurted. "It's new, and nobody knows who started it. They're totally against the rules!"

Mailee's expression grew serious. "Aren't slam books kind of . . . mean?" she asked quietly.

Audrey nearly choked on her mouthful of hot chocolate. Mailee thought her idea was cruel! "This one isn't," she blurted before she could stop herself. "It's just . . . harmless stuff . . ." she trailed off, and hid as well as she could behind her mug.

"She's right, this one isn't mean . . . at least not yet!" Elena giggled. "And they're *super*-fun. I did one at sleepover camp last summer." She had the book open on the table, and Lily was looking over her shoulder.

"Benjamin Carper hates green beans, and according to half the entries, Maria Pacheco has the best eyes," Lily read aloud.

"Julianne hates ice cream?" Nora cried, still leaning in. "What is wrong with that girl?"

"Maybe she's allergic," Mailee said thoughtfully. "My brother is allergic to chocolate, and he says he doesn't like it so people will stop giving it to him. He thinks it's easier than explaining."

"Interesting . . ." Nora murmured.

"I can't believe somebody started one of these at Humphrey," Iris said, shaking her head.

Nora gazed down at the page in front of her and laughed out loud at the list of disliked vegetables. "Wow, some vegetables are really getting a bad rap," she said, tucking a lock of blond hair behind an ear. "If I were a Brussels sprout I'd be furious."

"Or cauliflower!" Elena added. "Poor cauliflower has it rough!"

Everyone giggled and sipped their hot chocolate.

"So, if slam books are against the rules, why start one?" Mailee asked.

Audrey lifted her mug of hot chocolate and took a long sip. It burned all the way down.

chapter 8

"Hi, Mom, I'm home," Audrey bellowed as she came through the door. She stomped her feet on the mat in the front hall and pulled off her scarf.

"Hi, honey," her mom said, coming into the foyer and giving Audrey a kiss on the forehead. "Carmen called."

It hit her like a bolt of lightning, the shopping date she'd made — and missed — with her best friend. In all of the cocoa hubbub she'd completely forgotten! "Okay, thanks," she told her mom, hanging her coat and dashing past her up the stairs.

She was still reeling from Mailee's reaction to her creation and feeling a little bit stupid. Of course the nicest girl in the world would think slam books were mean! Thank goodness Elena had piped right up and said that this one wasn't.

Still, Audrey wasn't sure if Mailee would write in the slam book at all now. Her perfect plan could easily be turning into a total failure! And to top it all off, she had skipped out on her best friend. Audrey's feelings of excitement disappeared faster than her mug of chocolate. A sticky, guilty residue was all that remained.

"Dinner in fifteen minutes!" her mom called to her retreating back. "Dad and I are going to a movie."

Audrey knew that meant that she and Genevieve were signed up to babysit, but she paid no attention to this slightly bad news. It was nothing compared to letting her best friend down. Grabbing the phone off its cradle in the upstairs hall, Audrey stepped into her room. She hit speed dial number 3 (Gen's best friends were numbers 1 and 2), lay down on her bed, and prepared to grovel.

Carmen answered on the third ring.

"Carm? It's me. Oh my gosh, I'm so sorry. I totally forgot! I hope you got the jeans," Audrey spoke in a rush.

There was a moment of silence, and Audrey thought maybe she was really in for it. Or maybe she thought she *should* be in for it. Because truth be told, she wasn't *just* feeling bad about the missed shopping date. She still felt lousy about not telling Carmen her motive for making the slam book in the first place. And now she was so mortified she didn't even want to bring it up!

In the painful silence, Audrey considered telling Carmen where she had actually spent the afternoon but decided against it. Now was not the time. It would only hurt Carmen's feelings. But the secrets were piling up on her — and getting heavier all the time.

"It's no big," Carmen finally replied. But her voice didn't sound normal. It was, well, flat. "I got them," she added, sounding a little more upbeat. "They look great. And it's probably good for me to get used to shopping alone."

Alone? Audrey had no idea what Carmen was talking about. They'd been shopping partners forever, and missing a single shopping date was not going to change that.

Carmen was not usually a drama queen or the kind of person who liked to make you feel guilty. But she sounded kind of . . . lonely.

It has to be the volleyball, Audrey told herself. She should have seen this coming. Playing on a team had made her a lot less available. For the six hundredth time, or maybe the six millionth, Audrey wished that Carmen had gone out for the team, too.

Audrey chewed on the nail of her pinky finger while she talked. "The season won't last forever," she said, trying to console her friend.

"What season?" Carmen asked.

"Volleyball, silly!" Audrey laughed. Wasn't that what they were talking about?

"Oh, right. Volleyball," Carmen agreed, but she still didn't sound like her spunky self. Then, suddenly, she changed the subject. "So, how about that slam book?" she asked. "You've definitely caused a sensation. I just hope I get a chance to fill it in. You know, so people won't forget about me."

Audrey laughed. She loved Carmen's dry humor. "You're not exactly forgettable, Carm," she said. "And don't worry — we'll make sure it gets to you before you die."

After burgers with all the fixings, Audrey's parents rushed off to the movie, leaving the older girls in charge. Gen cleared the table while Audrey finished up the dishes and Dorrie pushed her "baby" — actually a stuffed moose with a chewed-up antler — around the house in a doll stroller.

"Soooo, did you solve your problem?" Gen asked as she put the milk back in the fridge. "Is the writing on the wall?" Gen hoisted herself onto the counter and looked at her younger sister expectantly.

"Well, I haven't defaced anything," Audrey replied, wringing out a sponge and wiping down the counter. She suddenly felt a little ill. "But I may as well have." She focused on a smudge of cheese and tried not to freak.

Gen swung her mismatched stockinged feet so they tapped against a cupboard door. "What do you mean?" she asked.

Audrey wiped a smudge of ketchup off the counter, then spilled her guts. "I started a slam book," she confessed.

Gen's feet slowed slightly and she broke into a wide smile. "Excellent," she said, clearly impressed. "I knew you had it in you."

For exactly half a second, Audrey was pleased that her sister didn't seem completely shocked. Maybe she wasn't as much of a middle-of-the-pack girl as she'd thought. But then she remembered Mailee's comments at the diner.

"Apparently, I did. But just this afternoon I found out that the new girl thinks slam books are mean. She might not even write in it! And if she finds out I started it, she'll never want to be my friend." The more she talked, the more Audrey felt like she might start to cry.

"What kind of a reaction are you getting from the other kids?" Gen asked.

Audrey shrugged. "Great, so far. Everyone is talking about it. About fourteen people had already filled it in when I saw it this afternoon. And the entries are hilarious."

"Well, there you go. It's a hit. And if everyone else is filling it in and having fun with it, the new girl will, too."

Audrey tossed the sponge into the sink with a flicker of hope. "You really think so?" she asked.

Genevieve nodded. "I know so. There's just one other thing. Does anyone know who started it?" She arched a plucked eyebrow.

Audrey shook her head firmly. "Only me, you, and Carmen."

Gen raised her other eyebrow for effect. "Good. You'd better keep it that way until that new girl gets it. Otherwise you'll never know the truth."

"Ow! You're going to yank my arm out of its socket!" Audrey squealed in mock pain as Carmen dragged her up the stairs and down the hall toward the third floor girls' room. It was first recess, and Carmen was on a mission.

"I need to talk to you alone," Carmen replied as she pushed open the door with her shoulder.

"Or . . . not."

Inside the taupe-and-white-tiled room, both girls stopped in their tracks. Normally, the third floor girls' room was deserted, but at the moment it was clearly occupied by a girl on her own mission. Girl: Isabel Collins. Mission: Filling in the slam book.

Audrey felt a little thrill of excitement when Isabel slammed the pages closed with a resounding slap the moment she heard them coming into the bathroom. The redhead looked up, startled, and breathed a sigh of relief when she saw her friends.

"Oh, it's you guys!" she greeted enthusiastically. "Have you *seen* this?" she thumped the cover of the notebook.

"Seen what?" Audrey played dumb, ignoring Carmen's look of surprise.

"This slam book! Listen to this list of weirdest dog names: Oogle, Beef, Munchausen, Speck, Rabid. . . ." She laughed out loud. "I mean, who names their dog Rabid?"

"Seriously," Carmen said, her voice sounding kind of hollow.

"That must be a new entry," Audrey burbled. "Did you see what Jed put for most embarrassing moment?"

Isabel's head shot up, and she looked at Audrey suspiciously. "Wait a sec. If you haven't seen this thing, how do you know what's in it?"

"'Cause she started it," Carmen said flatly.

Audrey shot her friend a "what did you do that for" look, but Carmen only had eyes for her nails.

Realizing a look wasn't enough, Audrey elbowed her friend. "No, I didn't," she retorted. This was supposed to be their secret!

Quickly, Carmen covered her mouth with a hand. "Right! I was just kidding," she backpedaled without gusto. "We, um, heard people talking is all. You know, notes have been flying about that thing."

Isabel saw through Carmen's too-casual tone, and the exchanged looks and elbowing sealed the deal. She stared at Audrey with wide eyes. "Wow, *you* did this?"

Audrey fleetingly wondered if Carmen had let the cat out of the bag on purpose. Not that it mattered, really. The game was up either way. "I guess I did," Audrey admitted, sliding onto the floor next to Isabel and pulling Carmen down with her. She could no longer hide the pride in her voice. She had done it and she was glad. The slam book was the most exciting thing to hit Humphrey in, well, ever. It was *way* better reading than science.

"But you can't tell anyone. If Mr. Sharpe finds out I'll be publicly humiliated."

"Yeah, and you'd have to include it in here under 'Most trouble you've ever been in . . .'" Isabel pointed at one of the newly added entry pages. Good one. There were several other new entries, too, including "Stupidest thing you've ever done . . ." Audrey hoped making the slam book wasn't hers.

The girls huddled over the book and flipped through the pages.

"Hey, look at this," Isabel said, leaning closer. "'Worst outfit worn to HHMS this year' — looks like Avery Curwin's eighties' jumper takes the cake."

"That's mean," Carmen murmured.

Audrey felt her blood run cold. Mean — just like Mailee had said.

"It's only one page," Isabel said, flipping forward. "And you have to admit — that was pretty bad." Audrey's stomach clenched and Isabel started to read some of the embarrassingly funny entries out loud. "I had no idea that David Ikonen's older brother shaved David's head while he was sleeping," she exclaimed with a howl.

"Or that he wore a wig to school for three months!" Carmen added. "But I always did think he had funny hair. Good one, Audrey."

The girls were all laughing now, which was a relief. But during the chuckles, Audrey casually pulled the book out of Isabel's hands. She was having fun, but they were getting really close to *the* page — and the reason she had made the book in the first place.

"Wait, wait." Carmen took the book back. "Let me see that. Can you believe Elena admits to biting her toenails?" Carmen asked, checking the name page and really getting into it.

"I have to stop laughing before I pee my pants!" Isabel said through her tears.

"Good thing we're in the bathroom," Audrey pointed out.

"Oh my gosh. Peeing your pants in the bathroom. That would definitely go under 'Most embarrassing experience . . .'" Carmen pointed at the page and the three girls broke into hysterics again. They were laughing so hard they barely heard the bell.

"We'd better get going," Audrey said when she could talk again. "We don't want to be late."

Isabel took the notebook back from Carmen and shoved it into her bag. "I'll have to finish writing in it later," she called as she rushed out of the room and down the hall. "And don't worry, Audrey. Your secret is safe with me!"

Chapter 9

"Audrey, excellent slam book!" a sixth grader named Daniel Rickford called out from across the hall.

"Love the dog names," added Everett Winnick, giving her a pat on the back.

Audrey brushed a lock of hair off her forehead and tried to look unfazed. It wasn't easy. Things were going from bad to worse! The school day was barely over and *everyone* knew she had created the book. Now, on top of everything else, Audrey would have to lie to the entire sixth grade class.

"Audrey, was it you?" Lily demanded, catching up to Audrey between classes.

"Of course not." Audrey laughed fakely. "I mean, can you imagine? Me? Breaking rules and starting a slam book? It's just a rumor!"

Lily looked confused but then nodded. "I thought it seemed weird," she admitted. "I mean, 'cause we were all talking about it at Easy Street and you didn't say anything."

"I *wish* I had started it," Audrey said, rubbing her sweaty palms on her jeans. That part was actually true, because in spite of everything else it felt amazing to have everyone congratulating her. It was like she had won an Oscar! It *was* warm in the spotlight after all. Only she was way too worried to bask, even for a second. If she wanted to avoid getting in trouble and find out what Mailee thought of her, there was only one course of action: Deny starting the book and get it into Mailee's hands, pronto.

Totally lost in her thoughts, Audrey didn't notice Carmen walking alongside her until she leaned in and whispered in her ear. "Guess what? I've got the book," she said excitedly, patting her gym bag. "I took a little peek, and it's filling up fast! There are at least four new entries since we saw it this morning. I'm going to write in it tonight — I can't wait!"

Carmen has the book. Carmen has the book! Audrey couldn't believe her luck. "Perfect!" Audrey cried. She pulled her friend to the side of the hall next to their locker. The fact that Carmen had gotten the book now was, as the last little window of hope for her plan was closing, like a dream come true.

"I need you to put the book in Mailee's gym bag while we're at practice so she can take it home," Audrey said.

Carmen's face fell like a deflating soufflé. "But you promi —"

"I know," Audrey said, cutting her off. "You can have it first thing in the morning."

"But I want to be number eleven." Carmen's shoulders slumped. "And I want to read it at home so I don't have to hide it under my desk."

"You can keep it as long as you want . . . tomorrow," Audrey insisted. "I just need you to —"

"Give it to the new girl," Carmen said. She emphasized "new girl," tilting her head back and forth when she said it. Then she shoved herself off the wall and heaved a sigh. "Why is getting it to Mailee so important, anyway?" she asked. Her dark eyes stared straight into Audrey's hazel ones.

Audrey looked away. This was her chance to tell Carmen all about her plan. "It . . . it just is,"

Audrey replied. She knew she should tell her friend the truth, but the words weren't coming out. Again. What if Carmen told her she was being stupid? What if she didn't keep it a secret? She'd already sort of spilled the beans once to Isabel.

The unspoken truth turned into a lump in Audrey's throat. She couldn't swallow it, and the two girls stood together at their locker in silence while kids clamored around them.

"Hey, Slam Girl," a girl named Eva called out on her way past.

"It's only a rumor," Audrey said, too quietly for Eva to hear.

"Whatever," Carmen ground the toe of her pom-pom-tie boot into the floor. "If it's really so important to you . . ."

Audrey broke into a smile. The lump finally went down and she patted her friend on the back. Carmen always came through. "Come into the locker room after we change. You can slip it into her gym bag as soon as the team clears out." Audrey looked around as she whispered, feeling like a special agent. "Mailee's bag is bright blue, and she always leaves it on the bench closest to the showers. Got it?" Audrey asked, backing up, already making her way toward the gym.

"Loud and clear," Carmen replied.

chapter 10

Even after Carmen agreed to put the book into Mailee's bag, Audrey felt jumpy. What if Mailee decided not to write in it? What if she thought it was too mean?

Remember what Gen said, Audrey told herself. *She knows about this stuff....* Trying to think positive, she hurried into the locker room and changed into her practice clothes so fast she got to the gym early for the first time in weeks! It seemed like forever before the other girls trickled into the gym, laughing and talking. Audrey wanted to hurry them along so Carmen could sneak in, but there was no way to do it without being totally obvious. So she adjusted the laces on her shoes about ten times instead.

When Mailee arrived, it was hard for Audrey to even look at her. She wasn't used to keeping secrets, and the effort was making her a little spazzy.

Mailee flashed Audrey a smile.

For the first time in days, Audrey allowed herself to imagine what it would be like to be friends with Mailee. She could totally see Carmen borrowing Mailee's turquoise-striped gym shorts for summer trips to the lake — Carmen looked great in blue. She pictured the three of them hanging out on the dock in the sunshine, laughing and talking. She wanted to tell Mailee that New England wasn't cold and snowy all the time — the other seasons were amazing! She and Carmen would show the California girl the ropes. They would be like the Three Musketeers, only better.

In her head, their friendship was practically sealed, but right now Audrey was so nervous she couldn't even tell Mailee how much she liked her shorts. As Coach Markham headed into the gym Audrey could feel the secret growing inside her.

"Three laps!" Coach called, and Audrey was ready. So ready, in fact, that she took the lead at the front of the pack.

"Wow, you're fast today." Mailee was suddenly beside her, panting to keep up.

Audrey smiled shyly at her flying feet. "I guess I'm in the mood for a run," she said as they rounded the first corner.

The only thing that could really mess up the plan now was Mailee believing the "rumor" about Audrey starting the slam book. Charging around the gym, Audrey waited nervously for Mailee to say something about creating the book, so she could deny it. But Mailee just ran along beside her in silence.

Audrey's mind reeled. Was it possible Mailee hadn't heard the gossip? Audrey hoped so. Even though it was clear that most of the sixth graders knew the truth, it almost made sense that Mailee didn't. Since she was in so many advanced classes, Mailee spent half her day with seventh graders, who probably didn't even know about the book . . . yet.

Ginger and Sandy picked up their pace a bit, coming up from behind and flanking Mailee and Audrey.

"Cute shorts," Sandy said. "Are they new?"

"My aunt sent them from California," Mailee told them. "Its waaay too cold for shorts outside, of course. But I figure I can wear them to practice.

Especially with Audrey pushing us to work up a sweat," she panted. "She's a speed demon today!"

Flattered, Audrey put on one more surge of speed and finished ahead of the pack. Behind her, the girls rounded the last corner and bent over to catch their breath.

"All right, I want six girls on either side of the net," Coach Markham called out. "I want solid bumps, clean sets, and strong spikes from all of you. We have a big game coming up, and I want everyone to be ready."

Audrey found a spot at the baseline with Elena and Ginger on either side of her. Mailee was in the front row next to Nora and a girl named Anna — which was good. Until she knew if Mailee really liked her or not, Audrey was happy to keep her distance.

Elena served, and before Audrey was even breathing normally, the ball came sailing toward her. She reached her arms out, realizing too late that her angle was all wrong. She connected with the ball and sent it flying against the wall.

"Adjust that angle, Jones," Coach called from the sidelines.

Audrey grimaced and waited for the next ball.

It was a long wait. When it finally came, she got the angle just right. Only she struck the ball with too much force and it whammed into one of the sprinkler pipes hanging near the ceiling. Ugh!

Audrey felt her face go hot as a couple of girls on the other side of the net giggled. "Nice *slam*," one of them said. Audrey looked toward Mailee, hoping: 1) she hadn't heard and 2) she'd give her a little encouragement. But Mailee was already returning another ball that Ginger had set up for her. They were both laughing.

Audrey looked away fast. She wasn't sure that they were laughing at her, or if she could take it if it turned out they were. The hopefulness, which had been growing inside her, flagged.

Mailee was getting more popular by the second, which meant that Audrey's chances of becoming her friend were shrinking. Soon they would be as small as a speck of dirt on the bottom of Audrey's gym shoes. Which was, as the on-court giggling continued, about how big Audrey was beginning to feel.

The whistle blew, signaling the end of practice.

"Get some rest the next few nights and make sure you eat well," Coach Markham called. "And don't forget to hydrate!"

The girls grabbed their water bottles and headed to their lockers. Audrey took a long swig and tried to focus on the slam book sitting in the new girl's bag.

Hurrying through the locker room door, she looked around for Carmen to make sure everything had gone according to plan — that the delivery was complete. Carmen was nowhere in sight, but Mailee's bag was sitting where it always sat on the bench, zipped up tight. Did she usually keep it closed? Audrey couldn't remember. She desperately wanted to yank the zipper back and peek inside, but the other girls were filing in.

"We've just got to beat Woodside," Sandy exclaimed as she plopped down on a bench. "Do you remember how bad the Wolverines creamed us last year?"

"Ugh, that was a terrible game," Anna added, slipping into her down jacket. "I can still see the snotty looks on their faces every time we lost the serve. . . . Ooh. It just kills me."

"We'll get 'em this time," Ginger said encouragingly. "It's our turn. Just wait and see."

Just wait and see. The words echoed in Audrey's head as she stared at the blue bag. She would have to do exactly that.

Easier said than done.

Chapter 11

Audrey was still in her room when she heard the unmistakable rumble of the bus turning onto Prospect Street. The clock confirmed what she already knew — it was 8:07 and she was way past late.

"Where's Carmen?" Gen called from the table as Audrey streaked past. "Is she sick or something?" Good question. Where was Carmen? Audrey depended on her best friend to help motivate her out the door in the mornings. Today she hadn't shown up to grab something warm to eat and race to the bus with her. In fact, she hadn't even called.

"What, no time for breakfast?" Gen teased, strolling into the foyer to watch Audrey flail.

Audrey glared as best she could while hopping around on one foot and tugging on her boots at the same time. As soon as her hands were free, Audrey grabbed a pair of gloves from the basket. Gen dodged deftly and grinned while Audrey pulled on her coat.

"Here's a muffin," her mom said, handing the paper-towel-wrapped pastry to Audrey. "You can eat it on the bus."

"Thanks, Mom," Audrey said, taking the muffin and yanking open the door.

Audrey darted into the cold with one boot lining still smashed under her heel. She shuffle-ran toward the stop, waving her arms wildly. She felt ridiculous, but if the driver saw her she would wait. And if she didn't, Audrey would have to tell her mom she needed a ride — something she tried to avoid at all costs.

Pushing her hat back, Audrey saw Carmen's boot disappearing up the steps. Then she saw the bus doors close.

"Wait!" Audrey gasped. Luckily, Ms. Lester didn't roll out. Audrey had been spotted and the driver was only closing out the cold while she waited for her to get closer.

Audrey's face burned in spite of the cold as she ran toward the idling bus. She knew that everyone on board was watching her, and she felt like a spastic bird. But she *had* to get on the bus today. Her mom would be furious if she asked for a ride, and besides, with a little luck, Mailee would be done with the slam book and ready for the world (or at least Audrey) to read her answers. Today was the day everything would finally come together. . . .

Ms. Lester gave Audrey a slightly disapproving look as she tromped up the three stairs and faced the long aisle of seats.

"Sorry," Audrey panted as she pulled off her hat and made her way to her favorite seat.

Carmen was sitting by the window.

"Right on time!" Audrey joked, sliding in beside her and unwrapping her scarf.

Carmen didn't look up.

"Where were you this morning? Did you forget to set your alarm, too?" Audrey asked.

"Something like that," Carmen replied. She already had her math homework out and didn't seem to be in the mood to talk.

Audrey took a bite of muffin and looked around. She leaned over Carmen to see out the window, thunked her boots together, and stared at her fingernails. Mailee was just two stops away.

"What'd you have for breakfast, a venti-triple-mocha-latte?" Carmen looked from Audrey's face to her twitching feet to her fidgeting fingers and back. "Are we a little caffeinated?"

Audrey's laugh came out like a bark. All four of their parents drank coffee. Audrey loved the smell, but Carmen knew she didn't touch the stuff. She was wired with excitement. For Carmen's sake she tried to stop herself from bouncing too much. "I think it's adrenaline," she said, taking another nibble of muffin. It was banana nut — her favorite — but she was too antsy to be hungry. Then she couldn't help asking, "Did everything go okay yesterday?"

"What do you mean?" Carmen tapped her math with the eraser end of her pencil.

"You know, with the *book*?" Audrey whispered.

Carmen erased one of her answers and wiped the page, sending eraser crumbs flying. She nodded without saying anything and Audrey tried to relax. It was one thing for Mailee to figure out that Audrey had created the slam book. It was another for her to find out that Audrey had it planted in her bag. That would be super-weird.

Taking a deep breath, she willed her legs to be still. Everything was going to be fine, just like Gen said.

The air brakes screeched again. The bus stopped, and Audrey felt her pulse start to race once more. She told herself not to be dumb. Mailee had the book, but she wasn't going to skip onto the bus, waving it around, and deliver it into Audrey's eagerly waiting hands. It was probably buried in her backpack.

Still, Audrey could not help staring at Mailee's hands and at her bag, hoping to catch a glimpse of the green notebook cover. There was nothing to see except that Mailee was wearing a new scarf.

"Wow. Did you make that, too?" Audrey asked when Mailee was two seats away.

"Yeah. Do you like it?" Mailee beamed.

Audrey nodded. The scarf was cute and matched the colorful hat everyone loved. She did like it, a lot. But what she really wanted to ask was: *Did you get the slam book? Did you fill it out? I hope you didn't think it was mean. So, what do you think of me?* Only that would give everything away and make her look even dorkier than running for the bus had done.

When the lunch bell rang, Audrey hurried to the cafeteria. Her ears were on high alert, listening for any talk of the slam book, and her eyes were forever scanning for the flash of a green notebook. So far, there had been no word, no sign. In fact, no one had mentioned it all morning. As dangerous as it was, she was going to have to do a little digging.

"So, have you filled it out yet?" Audrey asked a girl named Rachel in a hushed tone. She set her tray down on her usual table.

"Filled out what?" Rachel asked.

"The slam book!" Isabel hissed from the other side of the table. "Last I heard, over half the sixth grade had done it." Ever since the day in the girls' room, Isabel talked about the book like she was a bona fide expert.

"I was sort of hoping I'd get it soon." The voice behind Audrey made her jump.

It was Mailee! But what did she mean she hoped she got it soon? She should have already had it!

"Everyone says it's super-fun." Mailee sat down beside Audrey and tucked a blond curl behind her ear. For a few seconds, Audrey was speechless. She swallowed the bite of apple in her mouth and tried to catch Carmen's eye. Something had gone terribly wrong!

"So, uh, you haven't written in it yet?" Audrey asked, trying to sound casual.

Carmen seemed totally distracted by the nutrition information on her energy bar wrapper.

"Not yet." Mailee smiled. "But I'm ready for my turn. It'll be a great way for me to get to know everybody. Who's got it now?"

Audrey tried to ask Carmen the same question with her eyes. *Who's got it now?!* But Carmen wasn't looking. When she did finish studying her wrapper she acted as though she hadn't even heard the conversation. And when Audrey finally made eye contact, Carmen just looked back blankly.

"What?" she asked, looking over her shoulder.

Audrey jumped up from the table and tugged on Carmen's arm. Carmen didn't protest as she led her to the closest girls' room and checked the stalls to make sure they were the only ones in there. Her mind was racing. Could Carmen have put the book in the wrong bag? Did Mailee take her bag home without opening it?

"What, do I have something caught in my teeth?" Carmen asked, baring her pearly whites in front of the giant mirror.

"No," Audrey admitted. "Your teeth are fine." She let out an exasperated breath. "But listen. I need to know if you're sure you got the slam book into Mailee's bag. It was sitting on the last bench as you face the outside doors. It was the bright blue one that — "

"Hmmm. Wait. Blue," Carmen interrupted in a ditzy voice. She scratched her head and looked confused. "Is that the one in the rainbow between green and purple?"

Carmen got extra sarcastic when she was annoyed. Audrey had seen it hundreds of times, usually when her best friend was mad at her brother, August. She wasn't used to having that sarcasm directed at her.

"Of course. Sorry. I'm just freaking out," Audrey apologized. "The book really has to go to the right people. I mean, I could end up in a lot of trouble."

"Yeah, seems like I've heard that before . . . like, maybe when I said it." Carmen's sarcasm wasn't fading.

Neither was Audrey's rising panic. It was getting harder and harder to breathe. Carmen had put the book in the right bag, which meant that somebody else had taken it out. But who, and why?

And most important: Where was it now?

chapter 12

With a bathroom pass in hand, Audrey walked slowly along the west side of the school. The path to the restroom took her by the windows of two sixth grade rooms. Casually, she peaked inside as she passed. Nobody in Mr. Beaker's science classroom was scribbling under the desk. All was calm in Ms. Brackett's English class, too.

For a second, Audrey thought she saw a note pass from Bridget to Rachel and hoped it could be a clue. She pretended to drop her pencil so she could linger and get a better look. But when she paused to pick it up she saw that the flash of white being handed between the girls was really just a tissue.

Audrey raised her hand for a pass in her next class, too. Luckily, none of her friends — including Carmen, who was in Spanish with Mailee — were in this class. She didn't have to worry about asking for two passes in a row.

Cruising by the other sixth grade rooms was trickier. There was a bathroom really close to her French class. If she walked straight there she wouldn't see much of anything. So Audrey made up a story in her head and made a beeline for the locker rooms. If anyone asked she would say the bathroom near her class was closed for cleaning — a likely enough story. Harder to explain was why she was taking a detour all the way to the gym.

As soon as she stepped through the swinging door, Audrey could hear shouts and dribbling basketballs. A group of seventh graders had phys ed. In the locker room, girls' stuff was strewn all over. Audrey checked under benches and opened the lockers that weren't locked. Nothing. If the book had been here, it was in seventh grade hands now. Not ideal, but things could be worse.

Hustling back from the gym, Audrey strode down the wide hall and paused outside the door to the main office. There was a square window in the door. Audrey could see the school secretary's counter, where students picked up tardy slips. Beyond that was the principal's office.

Mr. Sharpe's desk sat behind a big wall of glass. There were blinds he could pull for privacy, but he only did that when he was dealing with angry parents or mediating a fight. Today the blinds were open. And something green was lying face up on his big metal desk.

Audrey felt her heart stop, lie still in her chest, and finally start pumping again like some sort of crazy locomotive. She must have been standing with her mouth hanging open, frozen and panicked, because Mr. Sharpe looked up from his phone call and gave her a funny look through the two panes of glass.

Audrey tried to smile. She also tried to see if the notebook was the slam book, but it was too far away and she didn't want the principal to see her ogling the stuff on his desk.

Nobody can prove I started it, she told herself. *Only Carmen knows for sure*. But her reassurances did not make her feel better. And she was still standing like a goon outside the office. *Walk*, Audrey commanded her feet. She could barely control her body. Horrible images swirled through her brain — being called to the office, put in detention, suspended, expelled, *humiliated*. She saw snickering students and wagging adult fingers — her parents, Mr. Moore, Coach Markham. . . . What if she got kicked off the volleyball team?

Suddenly, Audrey understood that the moment of warmth she felt in the spotlight — the thrill of starting something cool — could easily turn into a searing burn. It would ruin her chances of being Mailee's friend. She would be the girl who broke the rules for nothing. A few funny lines would be no laughing matter if they landed in the wrong hands. Hadn't Michael Narkis confessed to making TP wads and flooding the bathroom? If everyone's parents found out that Isabel and her friends stayed up watching DVDs *all* night at her sleepovers, would they stop letting girls come over? She wasn't sure. But she *was* sure that everyone would blame her. And she could see why.

Audrey's cheeks flamed redder than ever, but not from running. *There are lots of green notebooks in the world*, she told herself. *Just because he has one on his desk doesn't mean it's* the *one. It doesn't mean he knows.*

The slam book could still be at large, and she

might have time to find it. Nearing the door to her class, Audrey snuck one last look into another room — Spanish.

She didn't see any green notebooks or any kids working under their desks. But close to the window, she saw Carmen and Mailee with their heads together. Her heart gave a little flutter. *Maybe*, she thought, *Carmen was asking her about the slam book or telling her to check her gym bag.*

Carmen always had her back. Maybe everything was going to be okay after all.

For the rest of French class, Audrey told herself that Carmen was taking care of everything, and by the end of the day she believed it to be true. It was all going to be just fine because Mailee was going to take her turn with the book. Audrey was going to get her answer. And the three of them would be brand-new best friends forever and ever and ever. It was that simple.

"Did you find out if Mailee has the book?" Audrey blurted the question the moment she and Carmen had a private moment on the bus.

Carmen shook her head. Her face was grim. "I didn't ask," she grumbled.

Audrey could tell that she was worried. Even though Carmen had cautioned her against putting the book into circulation, her best friend would never want Audrey to get into trouble. That's why she hadn't wanted her to do it in the first place! Now she was probably feeling awful that she had flubbed the handoff, and Audrey felt bad that she'd asked her to do it.

"Hey, let's not worry about it," Audrey said. She put her hand on Carmen's shoulder to show she wasn't mad. "It doesn't matter," she added.

Slowly, Carmen turned to face her. She looked a teeny bit perkier. "It doesn't?" she asked.

"Nah." Audrey shook her head. "Nobody can prove I started it." She leaned in closer to Carmen and whispered conspiratorially. "I just hope Mailee finds it soon. I'm dying to read her answers!"

Carmen sat back hard against the seat and let her breath out through her nose. In spite of Audrey's assurances, she still seemed upset. *She's gotta have her processing time*, Audrey assured herself. Audrey nudged her a little with her elbow, and Carmen pulled away. That was okay. Audrey let her have her space. She knew Carmen would feel better when the book had been found.

They both would.

chapter 13

The next morning, Audrey's worried feeling was back. All night she'd dreamed that Mr. Sharpe was administering a test to her. It was one of those standardized tests where you fill in your answers with a number 2 pencil. But every question on the page asked: Did you start the slam book? And every answer choice was: yes.

Audrey tried to shake off the dreadful feeling. There was nothing she could do except hope that Mailee showed up at the game with the book in her bag. . . .

At least I don't have to catch the bus, Audrey consoled herself. This morning her dad would drive her to the game bus, which thankfully wouldn't leave without her.

Gathering her gear, Audrey quickly threw herself together. Her average good looks made it easy to be low-maintenance. She didn't have to fuss over herself or cover up any hideous warts or scars — a washed face, brushed teeth, hair combed into a quick ponytail, and she was good to go.

Gen was still snoring when Audrey passed her room, and Dorrie was miraculously sleeping, too. Her dad was sitting by himself at the table.

"Ready," Audrey announced.

"Aren't you going to have breakfast?" her dad asked. He pointed at the last three O's floating in his own cereal bowl.

"Coach said he'd have bagels for us on the bus. It's not good to get too full before the game." Audrey pulled her coat off the hook and waited for her dad to clear up. Truthfully, as tempting as the uncrowded breakfast table was, she could not have eaten if she had wanted to.

At 8:30, the Joneses' Volvo pulled into the empty school parking lot.

"Wow, there's nobody here," Audrey's dad said. "You sure you have a game? Are we in the right place?"

Audrey managed a laugh. The volleyball team had the same departure spot for all away games.

And there was one every other weekend from now until the end of the season. "Of course, Dad. We're just a little early."

Mr. Jones raised an eyebrow at his daughter. "You? Early?" he asked.

Her dad had a point. *If only Carmen could see me now!* Audrey thought as the bus pulled into the lot. *I'm actually waiting for a bus!*

"Sorry we can't make the game today," her father said. "But your mom has a deadline and I have to prepare for my conference. We'll catch the next one for sure."

"It's okay, Dad," Audrey replied. "Carmen will be there. And I'll see you later." Audrey climbed out of the wagon, waved her dad good-bye, and clambered aboard. She walked straight to her favorite seat and sat down, alone. Without Carmen in the mix the seat was all hers — and a little lonely. *At least she'll be at the game*, Audrey thought. After her nightmare night, she needed to see her biggest fan at the game more than ever. It was a bummer that the cheering section was not allowed on the team bus.

From her seat, Audrey watched station wagons and minivans pull in and out of the parking lot. Each one paused just long enough to deposit a teammate or two, who scampered aboard with packs and duffels. Ginger, Elena, Nora, Sandy . . . they were all there.

But no Mailee.

No slam book.

There were still a couple of girls missing when Coach Markham arrived with the bagels.

Coach studied the team list with his clipboard in one hand and his steaming coffee in the other. "Just a few more minutes and we'll get going."

Audrey gulped. *What if Mailee is late? What if she is sick?* Then it could be days before Audrey slept again. She kept her eyes on the window straining for a glimpse of Mailee's blue bag.

It wasn't easy to ignore the buzz inside the bus as everyone helped themselves to food. There was an almost electric energy in the air — it was going to be an exciting game.

A shadow passed over Audrey, and she looked up to see Ginger hovering over her. "Don't be nervous," the cocaptain said. She smiled her preteen-queen smile at Audrey, who, until this moment, had not realized she was jiggling her foot like crazy. Ginger probably thought Audrey was anxious about the game and wanted to deliver a team-captain pep talk. Audrey quickly grinned to set her at ease.

"I'm not nervous!" she enthused. It was a lie, but only partially. She wasn't nervous about the game, which is what Ginger had meant. "I'm good," she said, holding her foot still and slouching down in the seat in an attempt to look relaxed.

The look on Ginger's face didn't change, but she seemed satisfied. "Great," she chirped before turning her perky charms on somebody else. "Ooh, carbs! Good choice," she complimented Elena's bagel. "Perfect before a big game!"

Audrey bit her lip. *Um, duh? Wasn't that why Coach brought them?* Oddly enough, Ginger *had* actually set Audrey's mind at ease — if only for a moment — with the brief distraction. But now she was back to staring out the window and listening in on Coach Markham's conversation with the driver. They were going to leave any second!

Audrey had nearly given up hope when Mailee's mom pulled into the parking lot. Mailee climbed out of her station wagon, wearing a shiny, puffy parka and carrying her blue bag. She darted from car to bus without pausing.

"Hey, Mailee," Sandy called.

"Hey!" Mailee wheezed.

"Thank goodness you made it!" added Elena.

Mailee flashed a relieved smile at her team-mates. "We totally overslept," she explained to the coach. "My mom said we must still be on California time!"

"Well, we're glad you're here," Coach Markham replied. "Bagel?" He offered her a sesame with cream cheese.

Mailee nodded and took it from him before starting down the aisle.

She was just three rows away when Audrey grabbed her coat off the seat and slid closer to the window, leaving plenty of room for someone to sit next to her. It was an invitation — and Mailee looked at her for a second before plunking down in an empty spot a couple of rows up and slinging her bag into the seat in front of her.

Audrey's heart sank. She'd been hoping that at least Mailee's bag would be in view in case she got a chance to peek inside. And of course she *really* wanted Mailee to sit with her.

By the time the bus ground into gear and the team pulled out of the parking lot, Mailee was chattering away with Nora, Terry, and Elena.

"Wait until you see the Wolverines," Nora said, faking a chill.

"They sure have the right mascot," Elena said.

"Why's that?" Mailee asked.

"'Cause they're cute until they open their mouths." Elena bared her teeth to demonstrate.

"They're not so cute when they're knocking the ball down your throat, either," Ginger piped up from the back of the bus.

Everyone laughed. Audrey forced a smile. Mailee hadn't even looked her way since she got on the bus.

"Hey, don't forget Badgers are sharp, too!" Sandy said. There was a small cheer.

Mailee swung around in her seat to face her teammates. "Look, everybody, all we have to do is be on our game. Just ignore the nasty stuff and play your best." She looked at each of them in turn as she spoke — all of them but Audrey. Her eyes seemed to glide right past without pausing. Something was up.

When the bus finally arrived at Woodside, Audrey had a case of the game-day jitters *and* a feeling of doom. Since she hadn't been part of the team the previous year she had to take the other girls' word about how nasty the Woodside team was — and how good.

They changed in the boys' locker room since they were the "guests." When everyone was ready, Coach Markham sent the whole team to do a pair of warm-up laps. The bleachers in the gym were pretty crowded. Audrey scanned the faces — looking for Carmen — while she jogged. She needed her best friend to give Audrey one of her wry smiles or crack a really bad joke to make the butterflies in Audrey's stomach stop flapping around.

"Where is that girl?" Audrey wondered aloud.

"Who?" Elena asked.

"Carmen. She comes to every game," Audrey said.

"I thought she didn't like volleyball." Mailee was running just ahead. It was the first thing she'd said to Audrey all morning. She said it without turning around, though.

Audrey gulped. She didn't know Mailee was listening, and after being ignored on the bus, she was surprised she was talking to her. And how did she know about Carmen and volleyball?

"She doesn't like to play," Audrey agreed. "But she *does* like to cheer. And I think she's my lucky charm."

Mailee sucked in her bottom lip and finally glanced Audrey's way. "Maybe you should tell her that."

Before Audrey could ask what she meant, Coach Markham blew the whistle and the girls hustled over to the visitors' bench for a few last words before they took the court. "Stay alert," Coach Markham instructed. "And watch their serves — they're fast!"

The girls circled up, put their hands in the center, and pumped them up and down three times before ending with a shout of "Together!" Then the game was on.

Chewing on a thumbnail, Audrey watched the first half of the game from the bench. Each time the door to the gym opened she stared into the bright winter sun, hoping it was Carmen. It never was.

When she rotated in, the butterflies in her stomach had metamorphosed into something much larger — like pteradactyls with huge flapping wings. When her serve came — and the score was still tied 12–12 — the winged dinosaurs started to dive-bomb. She needed to hear Carmen yell her name from the stands — pronto! The only thing she actually *did* hear was her own ragged breath.

"You've got this, Jones!" Ginger coached from the net.

But she didn't. She walloped the ball and sent it flying.

"Out!" a girl with a high ponytail on the other side screeched. She threw her arms straight out behind her like she might get burned by the bad serve. The referee whistled and Audrey got the ball again. But her second serve was even worse.

A huge air ball sailed into Wolverine territory and they slammed it back at the Badgers' throats. No chance of return.

"Shake it off," Mailee told her. She was all business, though. No smile.

Audrey tried to remember everything she'd learned. She tossed the ball, hit it, and . . . this time it went over with a good amount of speed. The other team struggled to return it. But did.

It went back and forth until Ginger finally hit it out. They'd lost the serve. Audrey had lost the serve.

On the other side of the net, the Wolverines gloated. Nora and Elena had not been kidding about the snotty looks, either. The Woodside team was a pack of sore winners. They were good. *Mean*, but good.

Audrey was more concerned with what was happening on her side of the net — she had let her team down and she could feel the disappointment. If only Carmen had been in the crowd . . . If only Mailee had given her a little help, then things might have been different.

As it was, the Humphrey Badgers lost by two points. Two points! *The points I should have made*, Audrey thought as she slapped the other team's hands.

"Good game," she mumbled, making her way down the line of players. "Good game. Good game. Good game." *For you, maybe*, she thought.

When she climbed onto the bus, Iris was already sitting next to Mailee and the blue bag was shoved under a seat. The two of them were using a black Sharpie to make designs around the edges of their sneakers and didn't even look up.

Audrey slid into an empty seat behind Nora and propped her knees on the seat back. She didn't feel like talking, which seemed just fine with everyone else.

The phone rang once, twice, three times before August picked up.

"Hulloh?" Carmen's brother grunted.

"Uh, hey, is Carmen there?" Audrey asked. It was rare that Carmen's brother answered the phone. Like the Joneses, the Angelos had caller ID. August could tell when the call was going to be for his sister, and he usually just threw the receiver to her or at her.

"Carmen?" August asked as if he hadn't heard of his own sister. "Lemme see. CARMEN!" he shouted into the phone, then dropped it with a loud clunk.

When the buzzing in her ear stopped, Audrey thought she heard Carmen's voice in the background. She waited for her to pick up. But it was August who got back on the line. "Sorry, not here," he said. He hung up before Audrey could.

Disappointed, Audrey carried the phone back into the kitchen.

"Everything okay?" Audrey's dad asked. He had paperwork spread all over the table. Gen was there, too, poking a wooden spoon into the pots on the stove. It was spaghetti night. But Audrey wasn't hungry and didn't feel like talking.

"Yeah," she sighed. Only it really wasn't. She felt raw and exposed, like a rock climber on a cliff with a storm brewing.

Gen studied her sister's face. Her arched brows furrowed and her stained lips puckered. She gave Audrey a long stare. "How long until dinner?" she asked their dad, still staring.

Gen's intense look was making Audrey nervous.

"About twenty minutes," their dad answered.

"C'mon." Gen dropped her spoon into the sink and grabbed Audrey's hand. "Lemme paint your nails."

Chapter 14

On Monday morning, Audrey's fingernails were Perfectly Peacock and her mood was perfectly awful. Carmen had apparently been busy all weekend — too busy to call back — and Audrey had spent hours agonizing over her bungled game and the missing slam book. She needed to talk to Carmen!

To make matters worse, Carmen didn't come by in the morning and she wasn't on the bus. Audrey sat alone in their seat, slumping down as far as she could so Mailee and the other girls on the team wouldn't see her. Her plan worked. Nobody said as much as good morning.

Please don't let Carmen be sick today, Audrey pleaded silently as she trudged up the school stairs. *Please let her be waiting at the locker.* She reasoned that Carmen could have gotten a ride with her brother. August sometimes drove to school early for practice or morning detention or whatever, and sometimes Carmen and Audrey got dropped off at Humphrey. Carmen would usually call when they could catch a ride, but this morning Gen had been on the phone for-like-ever, and Audrey knew her sister usually ignored the call-waiting beep.

Rounding the last corner, Audrey's heart sank. No Carmen, just rows of kids banging lockers. No jet-black hair. No wry looks. No Monday morning jokes to help her out of her moody mood, which had just gotten worse. The prospect of a whole day without a best friend was totally depressing.

Audrey lingered a couple of minutes past the five-minute bell, just in case Carmen appeared. Then she hurriedly piled her books into the locker. She reached for the door, ready to bang the locker shut before anything could fall out. Too late. A notebook fell on her shoes. A green notebook. The slam book!

"Here it is!" Audrey said aloud, then looked around to see if anyone had heard. Everyone who wasn't already in class was rushing to get there. Nobody paid any attention.

Audrey quickly picked up the book and started to flip through the pages. It was like finding forgotten money in the pocket of your coat, or winning the lottery, or . . . Well, it was totally unexpected. And a total relief.

When the bell rang Audrey ignored it. She was busy. Right now she couldn't care less if she was late — she had the slam book back at last, safe and sound. And, upon closer inspection, she confirmed that it had some new entries.

Audrey heaved a sigh. The book hadn't disappeared after all. Somebody had had it and had been filling it out. And from the looks of it, the somebody had been . . . Mailee. Audrey's heart began to race. All of the fresh answers were written with a fat black Sharpie — just like the one Mailee had been using on the bus.

She had it all along, Audrey thought. *So why'd she act like she didn't?* Audrey's hands were practically shaking. The wide vents at the top of the lockers were just big enough for somebody to cram in a notebook. *If it was Mailee . . .* The back page would hold the answer. Audrey turned to it to read the name of the person who had written on line 37. All she found was a giant question mark. Then she flipped through until she found *the* page — the reason she had made the slam book in the first place.

In her own handwriting at the top she read: Audrey Jones is . . . A list of mostly boring answers followed: *Nice. A girl. Super-nice! A sweetie.*

The ink on line number 37 was bleeding through to the other pages, and when Audrey read it she felt like she was bleeding, too: Audrey Jones is: *A lousy friend and a terrible volleyball player.*

There it was in black and white: what Mailee really thought. And it was Audrey's worst nightmare. The lump in her throat swelled until Audrey was not sure she could breathe. Her eyes felt hot and her vision blurred. She had her answer at last, and the answer was so much worse than no.

Mailee had never wanted to be her friend. She probably only ever talked to her because she was hoping to improve Audrey's pathetic game, a strategy that obviously didn't work.

Wiping her face on her sweatshirt sleeve, Audrey blinked back more tears. This was the worst possible day for Carmen to be absent. Of all the days to be sick! *I wish I was home sick*, Audrey thought. She felt awful. Her stomach churned. Her head ached. All she wanted to do was climb into bed and hide under her covers.

Audrey clutched the slam book to her chest, flung her bag over her shoulder, and started toward the office. She stared at her shoes as she slowly made her way, working on her excuse. Nausea was always good, and at this point it was true. Her head pounded, but if she said "I have a headache" the nurse might just make her lie down in the office. She needed to go home.

"Hey, Audrey!"

Audrey's head snapped up. Mailee was coming toward her, calling and waving.

"Did you find your slam book?" Mailee was still far enough away that she practically had to shout, but close enough for Audrey to see that she was grinning. Isabel was walking with her — probably carrying the attendance sheet to the office — and when Mailee mentioned the slam book Isabel shushed her, throwing an elbow into Mailee's ribs, and giggled.

Great. Audrey pretended not to see them and ducked into the restroom. Isabel's laughter had sealed it. Audrey just knew they were laughing at her. And the way Mailee shouted? She must know the real truth about Audrey and the book, and she was probably trying to get her in trouble.

Audrey's red, puffy eyes stared back at her from the mirror. *Why?* Audrey wondered. Why had she been so desperate to be Mailee's friend? Why had she thought the girl was so nice? Why had she reached for something, well, higher? She should have known better. She should have known that leaving her safe spot in the middle would only land her on the bottom.

Chapter 15

The metal chair in the nurse's office was cold and squeaked on the floor every time Audrey moved. Ms. Phelps, the school nurse, seemed to be watching her to see if she was really sick. She'd checked for a temperature before she'd let Audrey call her mom, and when the thermometer registered normal her sympathy dried up.

Audrey's mom was surprised by the call. It was so early in the day she'd only had time to drop Dorrie off at preschool.

"Oh, Audrey, really?" her mom asked.

Audrey could hear the heavy sigh in her mom's voice. No, she could feel it, like a huge lead cloud hanging over her. Still, the answer was yes. Yes, she felt awful. Yes, she needed to go home.

Yes, she was going to absolutely die if she had to stay at school.

"Okay. I'm just going to swing by my office to grab some work I can do at home. Then I'll be right over," her mom told her. "Hang in there, honey."

As soon as her mom's voice softened, Audrey's guilt kicked in. Her mom was always worried about being behind at the office, even when she didn't have to stay home with a sick — or almost sick — child.

"Do you think we need to go to the doctor?" her mom asked, smoothing the hair off Audrey's face when they were in the car.

"I think I just need some sleep," Audrey mumbled. She slumped against the seat and tried to look pale.

What would really make her feel better was talking to somebody — fessing up — and for a moment she thought about telling her mom the truth. Then she saw the laptop case on the backseat and an accordion file folder next to it. Her mom's cell phone rang, and she slipped her headset into her ear and answered. Any thought of confession went out the window. Besides, if she told her mom what was really going on she would be in hot water at home as well as at school. This was something Audrey would have to deal with herself.

When they got to the house, Audrey headed straight up to her room. She crawled into bed without taking off her shoes and stared at the ceiling. A few minutes later, there was a knock on the door.

"Do you need anything?" her mother asked, crossing to her bed and feeling her forehead.

Yes! Audrey wanted to shout. *I need to crawl into a cave and stay there for a month! I need to move to a new town. I need Carmen!* But she knew none of those things were currently possible and also that her mom needed to get to work. "No, thanks. I'm just going to rest."

Her mom pulled the covers up to Audrey's chin and patted her arm. "I'll be right downstairs," she said.

Audrey listened to her receding footsteps as they padded down the hall. As soon as she was sure she was safely alone, Audrey pulled the slam book out of her backpack. Beginning with the first entry on the first page, Audrey read every word. But just as predicted, even the funny stuff did not seem so funny now, and she felt the tiny barbs hidden in a lot of the answers — not just the awful one about her. When she got to "her" page, her vision blurred and the words swirled. She wasn't sure why she had to see it again, but she did.

"A lousy friend . . ." Audrey gulped. *". . . a terrible volleyball player."*

Audrey's mind reeled. She hadn't seen Mailee's slam coming, not at all. She couldn't believe she'd thought Mailee was so nice. She wished she had never thought of the slam book. She'd tried to make a friend and wound up with an enemy. Total backfire.

She must have fallen asleep, because when Audrey rolled over it was almost 3:30 and Gen was standing in her doorway.

"What happened to you?" her sister asked. She took a step back, startled by Audrey's puffy eyes and rumpled hair, and then squinted and leaned closer. She lowered her voice. "Oh. Tell me you did *not* get slammed!"

Audrey didn't say anything. She didn't have to. Gen saw the book wedged under her pillow and stepped into the room, closing the door behind her.

"How bad?" she asked.

"Take a look," Audrey replied numbly.

Gen slid the book out and started to leaf through.

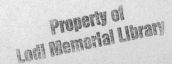

Feeling impatient, Audrey took the book, thumbed to the awful page, and handed it back. She watched Gen read her page.

"This isn't bad —" Gen started to say. Then she got to number 37 and flinched. "Who did it?" she asked next. Turning to the page of names at the back, she ran her finger down the list until she got to number 37 with its question mark for a name.

"Mailee. The new girl," Audrey answered. Her gaze lingered on the curled question mark. "At least I think it was her. . . ."

"Harsh." Gen shook her head in sympathy.

For a brash big sister, Gen was being really nice. Audrey barely heard her, though. She had just noticed that there was something really familiar about the question mark at number 37 — a certain little curlicue at the tail. It was something Audrey had seen a bazillion times before . . . on notes, cards, letters, homework. . . .

All of a sudden, Audrey knew. She tried to breathe and couldn't. She had that feeling you get when you fall from the monkey bars, land on your back, and can't draw air. The wind had been slammed out of her . . . by her best friend.

chapter 16

Audrey snatched the book out of her sister's hands, flipped back to the cruel entry, and stared at the words. She could see now how Carmen had tried to disguise her handwriting. But a few characteristic things — the curlicues, an open dot on every *i*, the funny way she made her *e*'s — gave her away.

"But why would my best friend write such awful things about me?"

"Your what?" Gen asked, clearly confused. "I thought you said it was Mailee."

Audrey shook her head as tears welled in her eyes. "It was Carmen. I just figured it out — the handwriting," she whispered.

Gen put a comforting arm around her sister's shoulders. "Did I ever tell you what happened when I created a slam book?" she asked gently, sitting down on the edge of Audrey's bed.

Audrey's head snapped up. "You started a slam book?"

Gen bit her lower lip. "Uh-huh," she confessed. "I was in seventh grade and bored to tears. I wanted to liven things up a little. So I started one with my then–best friend, Joelle."

Audrey waited, breathless, for her sister to go on. She remembered Joelle pretty well. She had spent a lot of time at the Joneses' house once upon a time. But it had been a long while since Audrey had seen her or even heard her name.

"It was great for about two days. Then people sort of stopped being nice. One girl, Miranda Sanderson, was so upset she didn't come to school for a week. Her mom told Mr. Sharpe about the book, and he demanded that it be turned in immediately. No one ratted me out, which was super-lucky. But slam books have been banned from Humphrey ever since. Joelle blamed me for the whole thing. We stopped talking for about a month, and things never really went back to normal."

Audrey sniffed. "I suppose I should be grateful the book didn't end up in Mr. Sharpe's office." She felt so stupid now and wondered why she ever thought that starting a slam book was a good idea.

"Chin up, Jones," Gen said with a smile. "Carmen has been your best friend forever, unlike me and Joelle. You two will work this out."

Audrey longed to believe her sister but knew it was too much to hope for. How could she forgive Carmen for this? She felt exhausted and rotten and done with talking. She offered up the best pretend smile she could muster and mumbled, "Yeah, maybe."

Audrey tossed and turned all night, her thoughts racing in a million different directions. At first she felt angry and more than a little betrayed. But the longer she lay awake, the more she could see what made Carmen do it and why she was mad at her. Ever since Mailee arrived at Humphrey, Audrey had pretty much forgotten how to be a good friend.

First, she had completely flaked on the shopping trip to the mall. She hadn't even told Carmen the truth about where she was! She'd been too preoccupied to ask about the secret Carmen had wanted to tell her — the one Audrey never had time to hear because she was too busy dealing with slam book issues. And the way she fussed over Mailee! Audrey felt her face grow warm in the darkness of her bedroom. When you added it all together Carmen had every right to be angry. Her best friend had totally taken her for granted.

Audrey didn't even know she'd fallen asleep until her alarm went off the next morning. Exhausted, she threw back her covers and sat up. She had a feeling that today was not going to be any better than the day before, but there was no way to avoid it. After pulling on the first pair of jeans she found in her drawer and a long-sleeved tee, she stumbled down the stairs.

"Oh, good, you're up," said her mother as she set a plate of scrambled eggs and toast in front of Genevieve, then crossed to kiss Audrey's forehead. "Are you feeling better?"

"Yeah," Audrey lied, sliding into her seat.

"You're looking pretty good for a sickie," Gen said. "Here, have these while they're hot." She slid her plate of food onto Audrey's place mat. "You want some juice?"

Audrey managed a smile for her older sister. "Yeah," she said. "Thanks."

"You can have my juicy," Dorrie offered, lifting her slightly slimy sippy cup to Audrey's face.

"No thanks, Dorrie," Audrey replied as she slipped some steaming eggs onto her fork. "You drink it."

Audrey ate her entire (warm) breakfast without being interrupted and carried her plate to the sink. She kissed her mom on the cheek before rushing into the hall. Slipping into her jacket and hefting her backpack onto her shoulder, she headed outside into the winter air.

Brrrr, she thought as she crunched down the driveway. It was cold today. She felt the knit hat stuffed in her pocket but didn't bother to put it on. Shivering her way to the curb, she kept her eyes on the thin layer of snow that had fallen the night before. She spotted Carmen's boots nearby on the sidewalk but forced herself not to look at her friend.

My ex-*friend*, Audrey corrected herself, hoping the bus would show up soon. *After the way I treated her, I don't deserve to call her my friend.* She wished more than anything that there was a way to make things right, but based on what Carmen wrote there was no going back. Carmen hated her now.

And nobody knew as well as Audrey how long it took Carmen to change tracks — and that was if she *wanted* to. The processing time on this? It could be forever.

When she couldn't stand it anymore, Audrey stole a look at her ex-friend. Carmen looked miserable. She had circles under her brown eyes and was frowning at the ground. It might have been a consolation, but it only made Audrey feel worse.

Finally, the bus rounded the corner and rumbled up to their stop. Audrey made a beeline to the edge of the curb and — amazingly — was the first one to climb aboard. Sliding into the seat right behind the driver, she scooched over to the window while the other kids filed past, oblivious to her misery.

Audrey stared out the window. The world looked so beautiful with its thin, fluffy white blanket of snow. All that sparkle made her feel even uglier inside.

As the bus rolled down the street, Audrey kept her eyes on the passing houses and cars and tried not to hear the conversation going on behind her. It was practically impossible.

"Did you read about Hank Perkins's most embarrassing moment?" a kid named Baxter asked with a laugh.

"Dude, of course," Liam, another sixth grader, replied. "Everyone knows his sister painted his toenails pink while he was eating breakfast in his flip-flops."

"Seriously?" Mac wanted to know.

"Dead seriously. I saw it in the slam book just the other day." Liam was convinced.

"That thing is awesome," Mac said. "I can't wait to get it so I can add my own stuff. . . ."

You can forget that, Audrey said to herself as the bus jerked to a halt at Mailee's stop. Audrey quickly turned her back toward the aisle and stared extra hard at the tracks that car tires were leaving in the snow.

She needn't have bothered. She heard Mailee stomp her boots as soon as she got on the bus, and, out of the corner of her eye, saw her stroll right on by as if Audrey wasn't even there. Sliding down until she was completely hidden by the back of the bus bench, she stared up at the ceiling. In only a week she'd gone from being in the middle of the pack to being entirely below "see" level.

Audrey was officially invisible.

Chapter 17

Audrey got to her feet before the bus lurched to a halt in front of Humphrey. With her backpack over her shoulder, she raced up the school steps two at a time. She didn't pause inside the doors to the building either. Or take her usual path to the locker she shared with Carmen. She sprinted up the stairs and into the girls' room at the end of the hall.

I really do have to pee, she told herself as she slipped into a stall and slid the latch firmly into its locked position. She wasn't hiding in the bathroom — not at all. She just didn't feel like seeing a bunch of people — or a couple of people in particular — right now.

The door swung open and a pair of girls walked

in. Audrey recognized their voices right away and lifted her feet off the floor.

"Where's Audrey this morning?" Nora asked. "I didn't see her in the hall."

"Not sure," Isabel replied as she turned on the water. "She wasn't on the bus either."

Yes I was! Audrey wanted to scream. *You just didn't see me because I'm invisible!*

"Well, I want to tell her I need a turn with the slam book, ASAP. Friends should have priority, dontcha think?"

Isabel laughed. "I guess I was lucky to get it early. But don't worry, it'll come your way. And the later you get it, the more fun it will be to read!"

Audrey was tempted to break out of her stall and interrupt the conversation with a news flash — the slam book was totally, completely over! — but she didn't want to make a scene. Besides, they had called her a friend, and it wasn't their fault that she had created such a dumb book for such a dumb reason. So she waited patiently until the girls' room was empty and came out of the stall to wash her hands. By the time they were dry, the second bell was ringing and she was late.

Throwing open the door, she raced down the hall to homeroom and silently prayed that Mr.

Moore was in a decent mood. The good news: Mr. Moore was running a few minutes later than Audrey and was not even there. The bad news: Everyone else was. The whole class was sitting at their desks, facing each other in the giant circle. And the only empty seat was the one she always sat in, right next to Carmen.

Yet another plan had backfired. Audrey had been so busy avoiding Carmen at their locker that she'd completely forgotten that everyone would leave a vacant seat next to her in their first class of the day!

Her face warm, Audrey crossed to the desk and sat down as quickly as she could. Carmen pretended to search for something in her book bag, her back to her ex-best friend.

"It's the Slamonator," Toby Mackenzie murmured as he erased his two hundredth pattern into another dirty desktop. (Toby was one of the few kids who regularly changed desks in homeroom to allow for the best possible pattern-making.) He gave her a sideways smile. "Your slam book is totally amazing," he complimented.

On the other side of her, Carmen snorted.

Audrey didn't say anything. What was there to say? The slam book had destroyed the most important friendship she had.

Still, she and Carmen seemed to be the only ones who had soured on the slam book. All morning, kids congratulated Audrey on her creation. Virtual strangers patted her on the back in the hall. Kids laughed together about the funniest entries. Pretty much everyone thought the slam book was the greatest thing ever.

Why didn't everyone realize that, in the end, slam books slammed people? Or that it hurt.

Audrey didn't even bother denying that she had started the book. At this point, suspension might not be so bad. But she did try to stay out of the limelight. All the attention she had been waiting to soak up was just making her feel worse.

With careful planning she was able to avoid running into Carmen at their locker. The problem was, a part of her didn't want to avoid Carmen. A part of her wanted Carmen to let her have it — she wanted to hear the truth about how awful she'd been. And all of her wanted her friend back. But that was impossible. . . .

Or was it? Gen's words echoed in Audrey's head. *You two will work it out*, she'd said. Could her older sister be right?

During fourth period Audrey considered her options. She could ask her parents to transfer her to another school or pretend she had some terrible communicable disease. Good options compared to suffering at Humphrey with her ex-friend. But no matter how she sliced it she'd be spending the rest of her life without Carmen.

By lunchtime, Audrey was ready to apologize to Carmen. No, she was ready to beg. Plead. Grovel. She would do whatever it took to win her friend back. She would even risk having Carmen scream at her in front of the whole school.

Maybe she'll even forgive me . . . in a year or so, Audrey thought hopefully as she walked into the lunchroom. She scanned the room for Carmen. When she spotted her in the lunch line her breath caught in her throat.

Carmen was next to Mailee at the front of the line, their heads close together as if they were whispering. Audrey felt a lump grow in her throat and her eyes begin to well up. Her mind flashed back to the day she had seen them in Spanish. Carmen must have told Mailee then about the slam book and what a lousy friend she was. It was clear as anything that they were sharing more secrets now — probably about her. And that neither of them needed her for a friend.

Audrey stood like a statue in the doorway to the lunchroom. She couldn't take her eyes off Carmen and Mailee. Laughing together, they filled their trays with food and carried them to their — her — regular table. They were so close their shoulders practically touched.

The room seemed to tilt as a wave of sadness passed over Audrey. She willed her legs to move. Turning around, she headed into the hall and made her blurry way to the locker room. She sat down in the farthest corner from the door, pulled the slam book out of her backpack, and flipped to the page with the horrible entry. She had something to add.

Audrey dug a pen out of her bag and, under the "Audrey Jones is" heading she wrote: *Really, really sorry.*

She walked over to the door, yanked it open, and threw the whole book into the giant garbage can in the hall.

Then she walked back to the corner bench and dissolved in a puddle of tears.

Chapter 18

Audrey blinked and tried to see the clock above the door through her tears. The hands were blurry black shadows, but she could see enough to confirm that lunch would be ending soon. She had approximately eight minutes to pull herself together.

You can't go home sick again, she told herself as she wiped her nose on the sleeve of her shirt. Gross, but easier than getting up for a tissue.

Audrey was staring at the streak of slime on her sleeve when the locker room door opened. Closing her eyes and leaning back against the locker, she hoped her invisibility curse was still working. Or that whoever it was would just leave her alone.

No such luck.

"There you are!" Mailee said, coming closer. "I've been looking all over for you."

Here it comes. Audrey braced herself for the onslaught as Mailee sat down beside her. Humphrey's new "nice" girl was about to tell Audrey what a rat she really was.

Audrey tried to breathe — in and out, in and out — but she could feel herself starting to panic. Carmen had no doubt told Mailee everything: how terribly she had treated her, how she was crazy to make friends with her because she was the new girl, and even how she created the slam book to find out if Mailee liked her. Because even though Audrey never told Carmen the whole truth about the book like she should have, Carmen probably saw right through the whole plan. She was no dummy.

Audrey opened her eyes but didn't have the courage to look at Mailee. She exhaled slowly. Her brilliant plan seemed incredibly lame now, not to mention completely desperate.

"Carmen swore me to secrecy," Mailee began. "But secrets have never been my strong point." Audrey turned her head, confused. Why had Carmen bothered keeping her secret now? "And I can see that you guys are totally torn up about this."

Understatement, Audrey thought silently.

"So I just have to say, Carmen really needs you right now." Mailee's voice was soft. It was not accusing, and she put her hand on Audrey's shoulder. "I wanted to tell you on Saturday, and I was afraid I would if I sat with you on the bus, so I kind of ignored you. Sorry."

Audrey was staring right at Mailee now. And she must have looked pretty lost, because Mailee giggled.

"Sorry. Again. I babble when I'm nervous. And I am kind of butting in, but here goes." Her eyebrows knit together and she looked super-serious. "Carmen needs to know that you will be there for her, no matter what."

"What are you talking about?" Audrey blurted, wiping away her tears.

"You know, if she has to move."

"Move? Move where? Why would she have to move?"

Just then, the door opened a second time and Carmen walked in. Her eyes were red and blotchy and her book bag was sliding off her shoulder. She was carrying the slam book, and it was open to THE page. Audrey cringed.

"I'm sorry, too!" Carmen blurted as her eyes

filled with tears. "I'm sorry I didn't tell you about my mom! I was waiting for you to ask, but . . ."

Audrey felt her eyes welling for what seemed like the hundredth time that day. But she was still perplexed. And worried. Was something terrible happening with Carmen's mom? "Ask what?"

Mailee jumped right in. "Carmen's mom lost her job," she explained.

"Remember that family meeting?" Carmen asked. "Well, it had nothing to do with August's inability to rinse dishes. My mom wanted to tell us that she'd been laid off. She's applying for new jobs, of course, but . . ." She sniffed.

"Most of them are far away," Mailee finished quietly.

"Oh, Carmen!" Audrey leaped to her feet and threw her arms around her friend. She couldn't imagine life without Carmen. Who would make her laugh? Or get her to the bus on time? Or find her math errors? "I am so sorry!"

Carmen squeezed her friend tightly. "I wanted to tell you." She sniffed again. "I really did. But you were so excited about your slam book. And then it started to seem like it wouldn't even matter if I had to move." She glanced quickly at Mailee. "You were already making new friends. . . ."

Audrey shook her head. She could see why it might have seemed that way to Carmen, but it just wasn't true. "Of course it would matter!" Audrey exclaimed through her own tears as she hugged Carmen for a second time. "You're my oldest and best friend in the world!"

chapter 19

"I can't believe we have to get late passes," Audrey said as she walked toward the school office. Making their way arm in arm, the trio moved in sync, with Audrey right smack in the middle. She felt like she had sucked a bucket of pool water through her nose — sort of washed and drained and a little woozy. But she was so happy that she and Carmen were back on track and that, after everything, she had a new friend in Mailee after all, she didn't care how flushed she felt or even how weird and blotchy she looked.

"It's so quiet," Mailee whispered, looking around the empty hallway. Their footsteps echoed as they walked together.

"Only the delinquents roam around when they're supposed to be in class," Carmen said with a giggle.

"Guess that makes us . . . rule breakers," Mailee said slyly.

Carmen looked around furtively. "Well, we do have a slam book creator in our midst," she whispered.

Mailee glanced down at the slam book that swung back and forth in her outside hand. "I can't believe you made this thing just to find out if I liked you," she said.

Audrey could feel her face turn bright red. "W-well . . ." she stammered. "I . . ."

"Wasn't it obvious I was trying to be friends? You were the first person to smile at me on the bus. And then we were on the same volleyball team. I actually thought maybe you didn't like me giving you so many pointers. I thought maybe you didn't want to be *my* friend."

Audrey stopped in her tracks. "Oh, no," she said. "I loved all your pointers — they were totally helpful! And I knew as soon as I saw you that I wanted to be friends."

"It's true," Carmen confirmed. "She was crazy about you even before she knew your name! I thought she was nuts going gaga for the new kid just because she was new. I had no idea you would turn out to be such a good listener. *Gracias, mi amiga.*"

Mailee giggled nervously. *"De nada."* She brushed off the compliment. "I just knew when I saw you and Carmen sitting in my favorite bus seat that the three of us would hit it off."

Audrey was shocked by what she was hearing. She had been so worried that Mailee didn't like her, and Mailee had been worried about the exact same thing! She spent all that time fretting and practically ignoring her oldest friend for absolutely nothing. Now it was exactly like she'd hoped: Three Amigas.

"I can't believe I got so wrapped up in that stupid book that I almost forgot about you," she said, squeezing Carmen's arm extra tight.

Carmen raised an eyebrow. "Swear you won't forget again?" she asked. She held out her little finger for a pinkie promise and the girls linked.

"Not even if you move all the way to California," Audrey vowed.

"Don't say that!" Carmen blurted. "That's my biggest fear."

"Moving can be scary," Mailee confirmed. "Ooooh, but if you move to San Francisco you will love, love, *love* my best friend, Cora." She was so

141

excited by this thought that she started skipping. Then, suddenly, she skidded to a halt.

"Hey, brain wave," she sing-songed, holding up the slam book. "I can send this to her so she can learn all about my new life in New England."

Audrey scowled at the spiral notebook that had been the cause of her own downward spiral. Then she shook her head. "I have a better idea," she said. "Let's give the book a final slam of its own."

Mailee and Carmen grinned and the three girls stopped in front of the large plastic recycling bin stationed in the hall. Mailee ceremoniously handed the slam book to Audrey, who took it and slam-dunked it into the bin.

"For good this time," she said with a grin.

Audrey's friends nodded in unison, then whole-heartedly agreed. "For good."

Check out

SUPER SWEET 13

by Helen Bernstein

Another
candy apple book . . .
just for you.

AN EXCERPT FROM

SUPER SWEET 13
by Helen Bernstein

"Now that I have a place for the party, I've got to come up with a theme." I pulled my straw up, then pushed it down through the tiny hole in the plastic smoothie lid. "'The party theme sets the tone,'" I said, reading a quote from one of the articles I had pasted in my party planning notebook.

"Plus, there are the centerpieces and party favors," Becca said, leaning over my shoulder. "At their party, Greg and Mindy had those stuffed animals and soccer balls in the center of the tables, remember?"

"Just please, no Fairytopia!" Lara blurted out.

I laughed so hard that I nearly choked on my smoothie gulp. "Oh, I'm not going to do that again!" I said after I recovered.

"Wow," Becca said, smiling. "I never would have pegged you for a Barbie girl."

"Oh, I was," I said. "But you'll be happy to know that I've moved on."

Becca smiled. "I was really into the Bratz." She covered her face with her hands. "And I still have a bunch of them in a box in my closet!" she confessed.

We all giggled.

"Hey, look," Becca said, pointing. "Ryan, Greg, and Max are here, too."

I followed Becca's finger and saw the three boys eating pizza at a table across the mall food court.

"Should we go over and say hello?" Becca went on.

Lara turned red, and I shook my head. It was one thing to send a party invitation to those boys. But it was a whole other thing to walk over to their table at the mall.

"Becca!" Lara whispered. "You're serious?"

Becca cocked her head to the side. "Why not?"

I could think of a thousand reasons why not, but apparently Becca wasn't considering any of them. She got up and headed toward the guys' table. Just when I thought she was going to make contact, she veered for the large orange trash can and dumped her Smoothie Shack cup in the garbage.

Lara and I laughed.

"Nice move," I said as Becca headed back to our table.

"I would have gone over," Becca said coyly, "if you would have come with me!"

As we watched, the boys got up and headed down the escalator.

"I bet they're going to the music store," Becca said.

"What about music for a theme?" Lara asked, suddenly inspired.

"That's a fantastic idea," Becca said.

Becca was really into music. Not only did she star in musicals at school, she also played the piano and the cello. I take piano lessons, but I don't play like she does. Becca was a natural. She could sit down at the piano and play a song that she had just heard on the radio.

"You could have big music notes and pictures of instruments as your centerpieces," Becca went on. "And you could burn a CD as a party favor!"

I nodded my head. "That's a good idea," I said slowly. "But that sounds like you, not me."

Lara and Becca nodded their heads in agreement.

"What about shopping?" Lara offered. "You could have shopping bags filled with clothes and cool stuff on the tables."

"Now, that definitely sounds like *you*!" I said, laughing.

Lara shrugged. "Maybe I'll do that for my

party, *if* I ever have a party." Lara pouted. "I hate being the youngest in our class. I won't turn thirteen until eighth grade!"

"What about animals?" Becca proposed. "You love animals. Especially dogs. That could be really cute. You could blow up a photo of Barney!"

Barney was my German shepherd. He was the sweetest dog, and I loved him. We got him when I was eight years old. Thinking about him made me smile.

"I thought about that," I said. "But it's too close to what Mindy and Greg did for their party. Remember they had pictures of Rufus, their dog? I want to be different."

"What about tennis?" Lara said, her blue eyes wide open. "That's so you!"

"The boys would all love it," Becca added.

"But it's not really glamorous," I said, chewing on my smoothie straw.

Lara nodded. "Ready to trade in your cleats for some high heels, huh?" A wide grin spread over her face.

I laughed. "Well, I'm not sure about heels, but I'm definitely not wearing cleats or sneakers to this party."

"This is kinda hard," Becca said, sighing. "But at least you're going to *have* a party. There's no way my parents are going to let me have one for my birthday." She took a long sip of her smoothie.

I smiled at my two best friends. "This party is for all of us," I said. "It's to start our thirteenth year, *together*."

I raised my smoothie cup to make a toast.

"Here's to turning thirteen!" I said happily. "And to a totally great party!"

"With a great theme!" Becca added.

"Maybe we should walk around for more inspiration," Lara said, standing up. "Shopping always inspires me." She slung her huge bucket pocketbook over her shoulder. Lara always had a bag with her that looked as if she were about to go on a sleepover. And the crazy thing was, she could find anything in there in five seconds flat.

"Good idea," I agreed. As I walked over to

the garbage can to throw away my smoothie cup, the answer to my problem was right in front of me. How could I not have thought of it before?

"She's definitely got an idea," Lara said, smiling. "Look, she's about to burst!"

"Spill it," Becca ordered.

Pointing straight ahead of us, I showed my friends the perfect theme. It was fun, colorful, cool, and definitely very me.

My friends followed my finger and saw the store that I was pointing to — Candy World — the biggest and brightest candy store in the mall. And by far, my favorite place.

"Carly's Candy!" Becca exclaimed.

Read them all!

Accidentally
Fabulous

Accidentally
Famous

Accidentally
Fooled

Accidentally
Friends

How to Be a Girly Girl
in Just Ten Days

Miss Popularity

Miss Popularity
Goes Camping

Making Waves

Juicy Gossip

Life, Starring Me!

Callie for President

Totally Crushed

Property of
Lodi Memorial Library

SCHOLASTIC

www.scholastic.com/candyapple

CANDY24

SCHOLASTIC and associated logos are trademarks and/or registered trademarks of Scholastic Inc.